"IF YOU GO TO TRINIDAD

YOU'LL BE KILLED.

THERE'S NO MONEY."

Sundance knew she could be lying. These people he was guiding, supposedly on a hunting trip, but actually on a search for treasure, were so full of twists and turns that everything they said had to be regarded with suspicion.

"You're giving me a good reason to duck out on you," he said. "But I'll get you away from here if I can. Then you can go to hell."

"Another hero," she hissed. "I'm sick of all you bloody heroes."

Sundance smiled. She was right about heroes— the world had too many of them, and not enough sensible cowards.

SUNDANCE #40

THE HUNTERS

Peter McCurtin

LEISURE BOOKS ❧ NEW YORK CITY

A LEISURE BOOK

Published by

Nordon Publications, Inc.
Two Park Avenue
New York, N.Y. 10016

Copyright © 1981 by Nordon Publications, Inc.

THE SUNDANCE SERIES

CHAPTER ONE

The bullet whanged off the rock next to his head, but he didn't think it was meant to kill him. It was too soon for that. Manning wouldn't want the hunt to end before it had even begun. Manning had come too far for an easy shot. Time and money had gone into this, and Manning would want to drive him until he was at his most dangerous: a cornered snarling beast blinded by the lust to kill his tormentor.

Sundance threw himself flat and began to crawl on his belly in the shale. He knew Manning couldn't see him now. But another bullet came close, as if Manning had figured out his movements. The bullet came from a long way back and there was no need to guess at the rifle it came from. It was a high-velocity, bolt-action Weatherby .300 fitted with a scope, a long-distance rifle with the flattest trajectory of any rifle ever made.

Sundance had handled the Weatherby, nodding his admiration while Manning looked on. That was yesterday.

Sundance lay still, waiting for another bullet to come. He had hunted many men in his time; now he was the hunted instead of the hunter. There was no fear, a useless emotion; all he felt was a keen animal awareness, a savage determination to stay alive. He touched the haft of the thick-bladed bowie knife, the only weapon Manning had allowed him to have. That was to give him a sporting chance, as Manning himself would say. Those with Manning watched, some narrow-eyed, some smiling, but all tense, while the Englishman searched him until he found the long skinning knife strapped to his leg.

Manning had called that "defanging the snake."

Lying on the rock-strewn slope, with the mountains ahead of him and the chill wind blowing down from the peaks, Sundance wondered if he had a chance of coming out of this. There might be if he could get far enough ahead to make a plan. Manning was good—the best— and he was the one to kill. If he could kill Manning the others would give it up, for this was the Englishman's idea of the ultimate sport. The hunting of a man as deadly as himself. There was nothing personal in it, no ill will of any kind. In other circumstances they might have been friends.

There wasn't much cover on the slope, but he hugged what he could find. The slope was bare close to the top and he had to decide whether to crawl or run. Crawling, he was still a target for a rifleman with a scope, and Manning had the best. A scope so powerful that it could pick up a fly on a rock. He guessed Manning could kill a fly on a rock, if the fly stayed still. He decided to run. He didn't jump to his feet but ran crouched like an Apache, springing from side to side, using his hands as well as his feet. The Weatherby boomed and boomed again, chipping rock, scattering shale, and then he was over the top of the ridge and running fast down the other side. At the bottom there was a stand of pine with juniper growing thick between the trees. He dove through a tangle of juniper and came up hard, grunting

8

as a sharp rock dug into his chest. Branches snapped at his face as he fought his way to the other side. The pines ran on for about a hundred yards and then began to thin out. No more shots came at him because Manning wasn't the kind to shoot without a target. With Manning there would be no lucky shots, no shooting at random and hoping to kill by chance. The slope dropped down again and ended in a brush-choked ravine that got deeper the farther he got into it. There was good cover here, at least for now, but if it came to a dead end, Manning would have him trapped. The others didn't matter.

In places rocks formed a wall across the ravine and he had to crawl over them, making a target until he was back in cover again. The ravine snaked and turned and grew deeper. Then there was a patch of blackthorn brush that ripped at his face, drawing blood and bringing pain. But all he did was to shield his eyes and move on as fast as he could. The ravine was now solid rock on both sides. The rock went up high and smooth and there were no footholds. But even if he could climb he would be exposed once he left the floor of the ravine. All Manning had to do was put the sights on him and blow him away. The expanding bullet with the solid base would send him crashing yards from where he was killed.

When Manning followed him into the ravine he would come alone. He would tell the others to stay back, and they would want to stay back, not wanting to face the blackthorn brush and the rocks. But Manning would follow no matter how bad or dangerous it got. The ravine might be alive with rattlers, but Manning would come anyway, to prove that he was afraid of nothing. There were things Sundance didn't know about

Manning. But he knew that much. There was nothing in it for the Englishman, not even glory, for he could never talk about it. The others would know though, and maybe he planned to kill them too.

Sundance rested behind a rock and looked back. There were no sounds and nothing to see. He didn't think there would be, not with a hunter as experienced as Manning, and when his breath came easy again he moved on toward the end of the ravine. And then he saw it, the blank rock wall that lay fifty yards ahead.

Motionless now, his eyes moved up the rock that blocked his escape. It rose up above the brush, sloping inward as it neared the top. It was cracked in places and a man could make his way to the top if he had time—if he had plenty of time and no one shooting at him, that is. He jerked his head around when he thought he heard something not too far behind him. It could be a falling rock or a branch snapping against another.

Sundance unscrewed the top of the canteen and drank two mouthfuls of water. He listened and heard nothing. High above him the wind whistled in the rocks, but that was all. He looked back at the rock and knew there wasn't a chance the way he was. Manning couldn't afford to let him get to the top. If he got all the way up, it would give him too much of a start. This time there would be no careful shooting, no putting bullets just close enough to make him lose his nerve.

Sundance stopped the canteen and hung it from his belt. Manning had given him the bowie, a canteen of water, and a handful of matches. That was to be his survival equipment.

Watching and listening, he stripped off his torn shirt and wrapped it around a rock. Then he struck a match and held it until the shirt began to burn. He waved the shirt until the flames burned bright in the shadows where he was. Then he threw it far back to where the brush grew thickest. When it fell the rifle boomed. By the time the echo rolled away the brush was burning fiercely, filling the ravine with smoke and fire. The smoke grew thicker as the fire ran back into the ravine, away from where he was.

Tensing all his muscles, he ran straight at the sloping rock wall, going up light and fast until he had to claw for a handhold to keep himself from falling back. His fingers dug into a crack in the rock and he hung on, kicking with his moccasined feet, searching for something to support him. Behind him the ravine burned and crackled. His feet took hold, and still holding on with one hand, he reached up with the other. Inch by inch, sometimes close to falling, he edged his way up the smooth rock. He made no attempt to look down at the fire, for every second wasted brought him a second closer to death. And then his fingers reached the top and he heaved his body over and rolled away into cover.

He lay there gasping behind a rock. The tips of his fingers were raw and bleeding and his chest still heaved from the tremendous effort. But he knew he had a chance now, and a little time. He could tell the fire was burning itself out; overhead the smoke was drifting instead of going straight up. He took a sip of water, drew the bowie knife and waited.

To climb the rock, Manning would have to sling the rifle. That would slow him—the Weatherby was heavy —and so would his boots. As soon as Manning's head showed he would put the bowie through his neck. There was no need to watch for Manning now. The sound of his boots on the rock would be warning enough. It wouldn't take the Englishman long to make his way through what was left of the fire. How long would it take him? Sundance guessed about ten minutes, then another ten minutes to get up the rock, burdened as he was by the big rifle, hampered as he was by the thick-soled boots.

He had to let Manning get to solid ground so he could take the rifle and ammunition after he killed him. It would be easier to cave in Manning's skull with a rock and let him drop back down, but if he did that he would have to climb to the bottom to get the rifle. Some of the others might be edging their way through the ravine by then, now that the fire had burned it clear of brush. They wouldn't have to be very good shots if they caught him halfway down the rockface.

And Baptiste, the half-breed, was a very good shot. He would be just as dead as Manning by the time the shooting stopped.

Ten minutes passed, and then twenty. That wasn't like Manning, who was a crafty hunter but not a cautious man. Maybe Manning was down there waiting for him to show his head so he could blow it off, though he thought Manning was after another kind of kill. He knew he could be wrong about everything.

He decided to give it another ten minutes. This was a good plan; he wasn't likely to find another as good. It was the first day of the hunt and he still had his strength. He had eaten well the day before. If the hunt went on too long he would grow weaker, unable to kill his meat. Unless he outdistance them by at least a day, he would have to live on berries or whatever he could grub out of the ground. There was some water in the mountains, but he couldn't take too much time to find it. So it was better to take a chance and finish it here.

Suddenly he stopped thinking as all his animal senses

became alert, sensing another kind of danger. Another man might have cursed himself, but all Sundance did was to sheath the bowie and start to run. He knew the Englishman had outguessed him.

He wasn't going to come.

Not this way.

CHAPTER TWO

Sundance didn't have to guess which one was Edward Manning when he came into the bar of the Trinidad Hotel. Just as he knew that the other Englishman was his brother. They might have been twins or just a year or two apart in age, but there the resemblance ended. There seemed to be a difference in the way they looked at the world. Edward Manning looked as if he owned it; his brother would have been content with just a fair share.

"You're Mr. Sundance, of course," Edward Manning said, getting up from the table, his hand outstretched. He had straw-colored hair, a clipped mustache of the same color, and the kind of fair skin that doesn't tan but gets trick red. The hump of muscle across his shoulders gave him a burly, almost awkward look, but he moved with an ease that belied it. He was about thirty-five.

"You're Mr. Manning?" Sundance said.

"No *misters* if you don't mind," Manning said, smiling. "We're all going on a hunt together. You don't want to be called mister, do you? Good. I'm glad that's settled. Sit down and have a drink."

Manning turned toward a dark-haired woman with a glass in front of her. "Sundance, I'd like you to meet

15

my wife, Alison.''

She nodded and Manning said, "And this is my brother, William. And that glum-looking fellow is Baptiste, my friend and man of all work of many years.''

Sundance shook hands with Manning's brother, but all Baptiste did was grunt and stare at Sundance with expressionless eyes. A French-Indian half-breed, Sundance guessed.

"Now what about that drink?" Edward Manning said. "The bar is surprisingly well-stocked for a place like this. Whiskey? Brandy? Anything?''

Sundance said he didn't drink. "But I'd like some coffee.''

Manning clicked his fingers at the bartender, who didn't like it. "Coffee for my friend," Manning said. "You're probably right not to drink, Sundance. I admit I do drink, but not for six weeks before I go on a hunt. Nothing worse than John Barleycorn to spoil the aim.''

Alison Manning said in her cool English voice, "Do you usually carry around all those weapons, Mr. Sundance?''

"Except when I take a bath," Sundance said. "Or when I go to bed.''

Manning laughed. "Don't mind Alison, Sundance. My wife is fascinated by your American Wild West. I confess so am I, although this is my first visit.''

"How do you like it?" Sundance asked, pouring a cup of coffee.

"When does it start getting wild?" Manning said, smiling. "I came here expecting to see shootings, lynchings, all that sort of thing. This place, Trinidad, is quieter than an Irish village on St. Patrick's Day.''

Sundance said, "The marshal here is a tough man and

16

doesn't allow it."

"Is he very dangerous?" Edward Manning seemed genuinely interested in how dangerous the marshal was.

"Dangerous when he has to be," Sundance said. "A few years ago he took on the McCargo brothers and killed all four of them."

"Yes," Manning said. "But how dangerous were the McCargo brothers? I mean, if they were just farmers or cowboys, what the marshal did wouldn't have been so extraordinary."

"The McCargos were the meanest killers in the Southwest at the time."

"That marshal must be very fast with a gun?"

"With a sawed-off shotgun."

"Ah yes," Manning said. "A sawed-off shotgun. That isn't quite the same thing, is it? Not quite as brave."

"He got it done," Sundance said. "He wasn't interested in showing how brave he was."

Manning looked puzzled. "I'm surprised to hear you say that. You of all people. I take that back. I'm not sure what I mean. Do you?"

"More or less," Sundance said, wanting to change the subject. He had come to Trinidad to guide Edward Manning and his party on a hunt, not to talk about courage. But he guessed Manning had plenty of that.

Alison Manning looked as if she'd been having more than one glass of brandy. "My husband is very brave," she said. "He's hunted dangerous animals all over the world and that makes him very brave. Don't you think so, Mr. Sundance?"

"I'm brave too," Sundance said, but no one laughed except Edward Manning.

"In fact, I have hunted all over the world, Sundance.

17

Africa. India. Burma. Now I'd like to go after grizzlies, bighorn sheep, mountain lions. But this country is completely unfamiliar to me. That's why you're here, Sundance. You've hunted in these mountains, of course?"

Sundance said yes. "If you're looking to shoot something dangerous, there's nothing worse than a grizzly. They look slow moving but they're on top of you before you know it. One swipe of a paw and you're dead."

"Just like a lion," Manning said. "There's nothing like it when a lion gets ready to charge. You think you know when they're going to charge, but you can't ever be sure. The trick is to catch them in the air. If you don't get them with the first shot, then it's all over for you."

Sundance said, "But don't you have natives with guns to back you up if you miss?"

Manning looked scornful. "Some hunters do it that way. I happen to think it's the coward's way. When you go out to kill a lion, it should be just the two of you. If the only object is to kill lions, why not shoot them from a log fort? Better still, why not just poison them?"

William Manning spoke for the first time. "Is there much big game in the mountains? Grizzlies, I mean."

"We'll have to go far in to meet any grizzlies," Sundance said. "The ranchers have been organizing big hunting parties in the lowlands. But they're in there all right. Far in and high up. How soon do you want to start?"

Edward Manning answered. "That's the kind of talk I like to hear. Half the time when you hire a guide you have to listen to stories of how bad the weather is going to be."

"I'm ready to start any time you are."

"Good man. Then we'll start first thing in the

18

morning. You'll have to tell us what we need. I suppose it won't be much different from what you need in any wild country."

"Not much," Sundance said. There was no need to talk about money. All that had been arranged by letter from England. The money was good—better than good —and he needed it. He liked Edward Manning well enough in spite of his tendency to say things that didn't have to be said. From what he'd heard of Manning, he expected him to be one of those tight-mouthed Englishmen, but when he thought about it, his own English father hadn't been like that either. Nicholas Sundance —his original name was never mentioned—had been an easy-going man who liked to talk.

As if reading his thoughts, Alison Manning said, "I'm told your father was English, Mr. Sundance."

"Don't pry," Edward Manning ordered. "Sundance isn't here to answer questions."

"It wasn't a question, Edward," she said, close to anger. "Not a question at all. A casual remark."

"Doesn't matter," Sundance said, wishing to hell they'd do their bickering in private. "My father was a remittance man. I don't know what it was he did, but his family paid him to stay away and he did. He took the first money they sent him. After that he wrote and told them to forget him. And they did."

Alison Manning nodded and the bartender brought her another drink. Her husband frowned, but she ignored him. "Then you come from a good family, Mr. Sundance?"

"Sure," Sundance said easily. "My mother was a Cheyenne princess."

"I meant in England. Have you ever been to England, Mr. Sundance?"

Sundance said no.

"Would you like to go there?"

Sundance said no.

"That makes us even," Alison Manning said. "I don't like to be here."

"I thought you were fascinated by the Wild West."

"I like to get my Wild West out of books."

Edward Manning cut in. "My wife doesn't like the reality of life, Sundance. Life is safe as long as it remains within the covers of a book. Oh well, enough talk for one evening. Are you coming to bed, my dear? You're tired. I think you should come to bed."

For a moment it seemed as if Alison Manning was about to say no. But all she did was shrug and get up from the table and take her drink with her as she followed her husband to the stairs. Without a word Baptiste got up and went after them. Only William Manning stayed.

"Are you sure you won't have a drink?" he asked, finishing his own drink and signaling for another. "It won't do you a bit of harm."

"No drink, thanks. Coffee was all I needed."

"Can't say the same for myself," William Manning said with a twisted grin. "I suppose you can't have missed the tension in the air?"

Sundance said it was none of his business.

William Manning said, "You seem to be more English than we are. Than my brother anyway. Edward believes in saying what's on his mind."

"What's on your mind?"

The question was put so abruptly that William Manning was startled. "Nothing really. Well, yes, perhaps there is. Are you sure you want to guide our party into the mountains?"

"I've been paid half the money," Sundance said. "I don't know what you mean."

"Oh, I'm not sure myself," Edward Manning said, staring into the glass that he had just emptied in one gulp. "If I may be frank, it hasn't been going too well from the beginning. I'm not as keen about big game hunting as Edward is. In point of fact, I haven't done any hunting since a lion nearly killed me in East Africa. Edward insists that this hunt will help me to regain my nerve."

Sundance said, "Not everybody likes to hunt. Why should they?"

William Manning looked grateful. "I wish you'd tell that to Edward. Edward says it's the measure of a man. All his life he's been bagging big game with that fellow Baptiste by his side."

"What does Baptiste do?" Sundance asked. Ordinarily he wouldn't have asked such a question. Right now William Manning was pushing the talk on him. There was something about Baptiste he didn't like. What it was he couldn't say, but the feeling was there.

"Baptiste came to England from Canada with a boat-load of horses for the cavalry. Edward was still serving then and somehow Baptiste attached himself to him. Edward paid him out of his own pocket, of course. After he resigned and took up big game hunting, he took Baptiste everywhere he went."

"As a gun bearer?"

"Yes, but much more than that. I've always thought that Baptiste got into some kind of serious trouble in Canada. Be that as it may, he's deeply attached to my brother. I'm ready to believe he'd kill for him if the occasion arose."

"He doesn't seem to like me," Sundance said.

William Manning ordered another drink. "Baptiste doesn't like anybody but my brother. I suppose he sees you as some kind of threat. Not that you are, but the man's half savage and thinks with his feelings."

"We'll get along if he keeps out of my way," Sundance said. "He takes care of the trophies?"

"He's very good at it. Edward showed him how to do it. Edward taught him how to shoot. He's good at that too. You're still sure you want to come along?"

"I said I did. You have anything else to say to me? Or were you saying anything at all?"

William Manning attempted to laugh. "Probably not. I worry too much, I suppose. Edward always says a man of action never worries. Don't mind me, Mr. Sundance. It's just the whiskey talking. Goodnight and I'll see you in the morning."

Sundance got the key to his room and went up to bed after he took his horse Eagle down to the livery stable. Later, lying on his bed, he thought about the party he was about to take far into the mountains. Edward Manning seemed to be all right in his swaggering way. The fact that he didn't get on with his wife meant nothing. And it was entirely possible that William Manning was nothing more than he said he was: a weak man who drank too much. Baptiste? He didn't know what to think about the Canadian half-breed. Only one thing was sure, and that was that Baptiste wouldn't do anything if Edward Manning didn't order it.

Yet for all William Manning's half-drunken talk, there was an unspoken warning that he couldn't ignore. It was there behind the nervous smiles, the things half said and then taken back, as if he knew he had gone too far. But it was too late to back out now. Edward Manning had sent him half the money and it was gone by now, transferred to the attorney who worked for him in Washington. It took so much money to fight the Indian Ring, and the other half of the money would be spent on the same cause. So there was nothing to do but go ahead with it.

In the morning they would start out early, heading for the foothills, and they wouldn't get there much before evening. The woman didn't look like she was used to any kind of hard travel. No matter. After all, what was the hurry? The grizzlies weren't going to run away. Sundance smiled and wondered how Edward Manning would take it when he faced his first grizzly. A grizzly was nothing like a lion or any of the other animals Manning had hunted. With a grizzly there would be no preliminary growling, no getting set to charge. A grizzly just up and charged, covering ground as fast as a running horse. In his time he had seen tougher men than Edward Manning start climbing trees when a grizzly appeared in all its fury. When it came to bagging grizzlies, as he called it, the Englishman might discover that he had bitten off more than he could chew. The momentum of a grizzly's charge could keep it coming, even when fatally wounded. Other big game might dodge off if possible, but a grizzly always went for the kill no matter what the odds. Manning might have read a lot about grizzlies, but in the end there was nothing to prepare a man for his first sight of the monster. There was something about men that drove the grizzly into a killing rage; it wasn't driven by hunger because it didn't eat what it killed. Once the enemy was dead, the grizzly ripped the body to shreds. After that it went looking for what it liked best: berries, roots, grubs.

There had been no time to tell Manning about the habits of the grizzly, not with all the bickering. On the way into the mountains he would tell him, at least try to tell him, but he wasn't sure that it would do any good. He wondered what kind of rifle Manning was going to use on the hunt. Most of the British hunters used what they called an express rifle or a double-barreled elephant gun that was more like a cannon than a rifle. His own rifle, to be used in emergencies—Manning was the hunter, Sundance the guide—was a .50 caliber Remington Rolling Block, a single-shot that fired a bullet powered by seventy grains of black powder. It was heavy and dependable and it loaded by thumbing the hammer to full cock and then rolling back the block to expose the breech. You pushed in a cartridge, flipped the block back into place, and it was ready to fire. After you got used to the way it loaded and unloaded, you went through the motions without thinking. It was a good rifle for killing men and animals at long distance. His other long gun, the .44-40 Winchester, took the same cartridges as his long-barreled, single-action Colt, which made it unnecessary to carry two kinds of ammunition. The rest of the weapons were all part of his personal arsenal: straight-handled throwing hatchet, big bowie knife with a ten-inch blade, and skinning knife that he carried in a sheath strapped to his leg. All these weapons had saved his life at one time or another. Like the great stallion Eagle, they were part of his life as a professional fighting man.

The hunt was to last for two weeks, and for that he would be paid two thousand dollars, more money than he could have earned at any kind of work short of holding up banks. Without conceit, Sundance knew he was good at what he did. Even so, there were men who were just as good when it came to acting as a guide for a hunting party. Old Ike Murphy, often called the last of the mountain men and still tough as leather at seventy, would have been glad to do it for half the money. Otto Moyler, ever broke because he was mad for poker and played it badly, would have jumped at the chance to make five hundred for two weeks of walking over the mountains. So why hadn't Manning hired Murphy or Moyler? As guides they were better known than he was. Old Ike even had a dime novel written about his exploits. It was still on sale in railroad depots and cigar stores all over the country.

It could be that Manning didn't care about money, of which he had plenty. Yet it was a fact that rich people didn't throw their money around too freely. Maybe this rich man was different from the others. After all he was a hunter and hunters were a reckless breed, especially this one, if you could go by appearances. If it hadn't been for the brother's talk earlier in the evening, Sundance would not have concerned himself with Manning's reasons for hiring him. He was not concerned now, but he was thinking about it. If there was an answer he didn't find it, and so he went to sleep.

Manning was up before he was, and when Sundance went downstairs he found him eating breakfast in the bar. The sun wasn't up yet and there was no one there but the day bartender who doubled as cook. It was quiet in the hotel and in the street outside, and thought it was chilly now it would be baking hot in a few hours.

"Dig in," Manning said heartily, forking another steak onto his plate. "You like fried eggs with your steak? That's all they eat for breakfast in Australia."

"We do it here too," Sundance said, drinking his first cup of coffee of the day. He put two eggs on top of his

25

steak and used plenty of salt and pepper.

"I trust you slept well," Manning said. "I always do. Most people worry themselves to sleep, then do nothing about their worries when they wake up. I'm quite the opposite. I don't worry, but I do get things done. One thing at a time is my motto."

"Sure," Sundance said, reaching for the coffee pot. "We're going to need tents and plenty of blankets. It'll be cold where we're going."

Manning waved his hand. "I leave all that to you. Spend what you like. I won't be hunting after this trip."

"You mean you're quitting?"

"Yes, I've had enough of it. When something starts to get stale it's time to give it up. Does that surprise you?"

"Why should it? From what I hear you've been a big success at it."

Manning nodded. "That's what they tell me. What most people don't know is that the animal really doesn't have much of a chance. Accidents do happen, I suppose, but they've never happened to me. This last year or so I've been giving the animals odds and I still kill them."

"What kind of odds?" Sundance asked.

"Letting them get closer, shooting at the last second, that sort of thing. I haven't even been scratched. That's a stupid thing to say. What I mean is, I'm still alive. Come to think of it, you're still alive."

Sundance smiled. "I don't give odds."

"But you do take chances?"

"When I have to. It's not the same thing."

"In a way, it is. You could do something else besides what you do."

"I'll quit when I get too old for it," Sundance said.

26

"You think you'll live to be old?" Manning asked.

"That's my intention." That wasn't true, Sundance realized, but he'd be damned if he'd talk about something that was none of Manning's business.

"I don't think I'd like to be old," Manning said. "I'm thirty-six now. I look upon age as a disease that can't be arrested."

"You'll get used to it when the time comes," Sundance said. "Most people do."

"I don't care what most people do."

"Most people are most people." Sundance wished the others would come down to breakfast. Still, the more a man talked, the more you knew about him, though he wasn't sure that everything Manning said was what he felt.

"You're not just any man," Manning said. "Neither am I. So why pretend that we are. I know more about you than you think. Oh, I haven't been snooping around behind your back and I haven't hired detectives to give me your life's history. The things you've done are common knowledge."

"You give me too much credit," Sundance said.

"Not a bit," Manning said. "Your battles with these politicians—this Indian Ring—is unique in my experience. They want to kill you, but they haven't been able to do it. They've killed other men, haven't they? I know they have, yet they haven't been able to kill you. That makes you different."

"Not so different," Sundance said. "If I could fight them any other way I'd do it. I'm not a lawyer so I have to pay Washington lawyers to do the talking. That takes money. I get it with my guns."

Manning looked at Sundance's copper skin and shoulder-length yellow hair, his pale blue eyes, his buckskins, the weapons he carried slung from his belt. "I can't see you arguing a case in front of the Supreme Court," he said. "I think you'd be a washout as a lawyer. No offense?"

"No offense. I'd be a lousy lawyer."

"But you could be a lawyer if you set your mind to it. Older men than you have become lawyers, especially in this country where the rules aren't so strict. How long would it take you to read law in a lawyer's office? That's one way of doing it, I'm told. You're a highly intelligent man. In a year or two you could be a full-fledged lawyer. But you won't do it because you prefer the life you live now. All the danger, all the killing —that's what you like best."

Manning laughed and Sundance smiled back at him. "You should have been a lawyer yourself. You always talk so much this early in the morning?"

"Only to men who know what I'm talking about."

"But not women?"

"Women have their uses, but you can't talk to them because they aren't logical. They make everything so personal. You try to discuss an idea—any idea—and they wonder: 'How do I fit in?' And speaking of the ladies, here comes my dear wife."

Looking as if she hadn't slept at all, Alison Manning came down the stairs followed by Baptiste. Before she sat down she bent her head and allowed Manning to kiss her on the cheek.

"You look very well this morning, my dear," Manning said.

"Good morning, Mr. Sundance," was all she said. "Will you pour me some coffee?"

Manning smiled broadly while the coffee was poured.

In a few minutes, William Manning came down and

said all he wanted was coffee. He filled half his cup, then topped it with whiskey. "Hair of the dog," he said, trying to make a joke of it.

"Your dog keeps getting bigger," Edward Manning said. "One of these days you aren't going to be able to bite him back. You don't want to have shaky hands when some grizzly bear comes charging at you, do you?"

William finished his fortified coffee and looked at his brother. "I think I'll leave the grizzlies to you, Edward. You're the hunter. You do the hunting."

"Nonsense," said Edward Manning. "What you're saying is just too generous and I won't hear of it. Of course you're going to hunt grizzly bears. You've heard too many stories about them, that's all it is. Once you're out in the cold, crisp air of the mountains you'll feel like a new man. Isn't that right, Sundance?"

"We'll all be cold if we climb high enough," Sundance said.

Looking neither right nor left, Baptiste was eating noisily, forking meat into his mouth until his cheeks bulged, holding the coffee cup as if it didn't have a handle.

Alison Manning regarded him with disgust until finally her anger broke loose. "For God's sake, Edward, why does he have to eat with us?"

In turn, Edward Manning regarded her with cold, hard eyes. "Because he does, that's why. Because I told him he could."

Baptiste went on eating as if he hadn't heard.

"I hope you don't mind," Edward Manning said. "I hope you don't mind, because it won't make any difference if you do."

"Thank you," she said. "But what does it prove?"

"It proves that Baptiste isn't just my servant. He's my friend." Manning turned in his chair and raised his voice. "You there, bartender. Do you mind sweeping out this place some other time? We're having breakfast and you're raising dust."

The bartender, an elderly man, stood his ground. "Ain't no dust, mister. This sawdust is still damp. Nobody's keeping you from your breakfast, but I got work to do."

Edward Manning clicked his fingers at Baptiste. "Make him stop."

Baptiste heaved his bulk out of the chair and Sundance said, "Call him off, Manning. This isn't England. Let the man do his work."

"Wait, Baptiste," Manning said, as if talking to a trained dog. Baptiste's dark eyes moved to Sundance.

Manning smiled and said, "You think you could stop my man, Sundance?"

Sundance nodded. "I think so," he said, ready to drop Baptiste with a bullet in the leg if he came at him. Baptiste was as tall as he was, and maybe fifty pounds heavier, and he wasn't about to roll around in the sawdust on a barroom floor just to give Manning whatever satisfaction he got out of this.

"What is all this foolishness?" William Manning said in a nervous rush of words. "I don't see any dust. What is all this talk about dust?"

"This isn't about dust," Edward Manning said. "Drink your breakfast, William. Keep out of this."

Rattled by the way things were going, the bartender went back behind the bar and put the broom away.

Edward Manning smiled. "There you see, it's all settled. Sit down, Baptiste. Finish your meal." Baptiste hesitated and Manning clicked his fingers. "I told you

30

to sit down.''

Sundance got up and said he was going to see about the supplies. Manning followed him outside and told him to hold up for a minute. Sundance turned to face him.

"Just out of curiosity," Manning said. "Would you really have gone against my man just because of a stupid bartender? You don't even know him."

"He's an old man," Sundance said. "I don't have to know him. It's that simple."

Manning shook his head. "No," he said. "Nothing is ever simple."

CHAPTER THREE

By the time they were ready to leave, Edward Manning was wearing a big .455 Webley revolver in a bullet-looped belt and the pack ponies were loaded down with tents and supplies. Trinidad was wide awake now and the townspeople had gathered to see them off. Manning, in laced boots and a wide-brimmed hat with a leopard skin band, attracted as much attention as Sundance in his buckskins. William Manning wore laced boots too; his hat was just a hat. In the sunlight his freckled face had a sickly tinge. He wasn't wearing a belt gun.

They mounted up and Baptiste led the pack ponies. Alison Manning knew how to handle a horse, though the Western saddle was not to her liking. She wore a Webley like her husband, but in a smaller caliber, and there was no way to tell how well she could use it. Sundance guessed she was a fair hand with a gun.

Sundance carried the .50 caliber Remington tied across the back of his saddle. It was too big a rifle to be carried under his leg. The rest of the rifles were packed on the ponies.

"I don't suppose we'll have anything decent to shoot for a few days," Manning said as they started out.

"Not in the lowlands," Sundance said. "Bobcats,

mule deer, a few coyotes. What you're looking for is always high up. A few years back a mountain lion with a bullet healed up in him started making raids on the stockmen. I guess the animal was in a lot of pain. Maybe it was rabid as well. I don't know because I wasn't there. They had to cordon off the whole country before they scored a kill."

"I wish I could have seen that," Manning said. "Do grizzlies ever get rabies?"

"All animals do. It hardly makes any difference with a grizzly. He'll come after you no matter how he's feeling. You may try to run. He can run faster."

"What about bighorn sheep? They tell me they're dying out."

"Not yet but they're dwindling. It's like with the buffalo. They've been overhunted. Now you have to go clear up to the peaks to find them. You mean to go that high? If you do there can't be any tents. If you want to go, we can set up a base camp and hunt from there."

"Bighorns aren't very dangerous, are they?"

"No. Getting to where you can kill them is harder than killing them. The rams will fight if cornered. That's all."

"Mountain lions?"

"They stay clear of man unless they turn killer. I've heard of a few cases. Probably just stories. The big ones weigh up to two hundred pounds. But they run when they can."

"A pity," Manning said. "That leaves the grizzly. You've hunted them?"

"I've killed just one," Sundance said. "The bear was trying to kill me."

"You haven't hunted much for sport, have you?"

"I have a good friend who likes to hunt for sport.

He's a soldier who doesn't like to kill people. If you're asking me if I like to hunt for sport, the answer is yes. But I don't seem to find the time."

"You have the time now," Manning said.

Sundance noticed that Manning's brother kept sipping at his canteen. Either he was thirsty or there was something in the canteen besides water. So far there was enough water, so Sundance didn't say anything. On the trail a guide took orders from the man who was employing him, and that held true until somebody's behavior put the whole party in danger. Then the guide became boss if he had the guts to enforce his decisions. Sundance wondered if it would come to that.

West of Trinidad the country was sparsely settled. Mostly it was cow country, but there were farms where the water was good. The foothills rolled on ahead of them. Beyond the hills, jagged against the sky, were the mountains, the tail end of the Rockies, wild country only haphazardly explored by Fremont more than thirty years before. Their destination was the Four Corners where Utah, Colorado, Arizona and New Mexico met. The Spaniards, who hadn't been told that it couldn't be done, had crossed the mountains now known as the Four Corners. Three hundred years later Fremond had passed that way. Nothing had changed during all those years, except that there were rumors of a bandit hideout somewhere in the Corners. Sundance didn't put much stock in rumors, yet it was possible that there were hard-hunted outlaws holed up in there, fanning out to the four states and territories when they thought it was safe.

By noon they were twenty miles from Trinidad and the sun was at its hottest, but Manning, accustomed to India and Africa, took it in his stride. In fact, the only one who showed signs of wear was Manning's brother.

His color hadn't improved and he was sweating hard. He continued to sip from his canteen all through the meal. While the others ate he just pushed the food around on his plate.

Edward Manning ate like a boy on a picnic, going for second helpings of everything. Baptiste kept filling Manning's cup with black coffee heaped with brown sugar and condensed milk. The fire, made of pine, burned pale in the harsh sunlight, giving off a pleasant resiny smell. The hill where they made camp was covered with columbines and asters. William Manning, giving up on his food, scraped out his plate and unstoppered his canteen. Now and then Alison Manning looked at him, but said nothing.

Manning lit his pipe and looked at the mountains still many miles away. "Will we be there," he pointed with the pipe stem, "sometime tomorrow?"

Sundance said, "By midday if we make an early start."

"My husband can't wait to start killing," Alison Manning said, not looking at anyone in particular.

"Why not, my dear?" Manning said, ignoring the bitterness in her voice. "It's going to be my last hunt, after all."

Alison Manning's eyes jumped to him. "Did you say your last hunt? Is this another of your jokes, or do you mean it?"

"It's not a joke. This is my last time out."

"But why haven't you said something before this?"

"I wanted it to be a surprise. Aren't you happy about it?"

Alison Manning was flustered in spite of her effort to regain control of herself. "Of course I'm happy, Edward. It's just that I never dreamt—"

"That I'd give up so soon? Well, why not? Everything comes to an end. Everything."

William Manning swigged hard at his canteen and said with false good humor, "Since you're decided to pack it in, why not do it right now? Let's make this a camping trip? Don't you think that's a good idea, Sundance?"

Sundance shrugged. "That's not for me to say."

"Of course it isn't," Edward Manning agreed. He made a face. "I haven't been on a camping trip since I was a boy. What would you like me to do, William? Collect butterflies? Shiny stones? Interesting leaves to be pressed flat in books?"

"It was just a thought," his brother said.

"And not a very good one," Manning said. "Now don't get sulky because you've had too much to drink. Cheer up, old man. It's a fine day and we're going to have a fine time. Tonight we'll sleep under canvas and in the morning we'll be in the mountains."

"You can keep the damned mountains," William Manning said, brave with whiskey. "I'd just as soon be home in England."

Manning tapped out his pipe on the heel of his boot. "Ah yes," he said. "Our tame little English hills. Come on, you people. It's time we traveled on with the sun."

That night, just before dark, they made camp by a shallow creek with cottonwoods growing along its banks. Sundance, Baptiste and Manning set up the two tents, one for Manning and his wife, the other for Manning's brother. When the tents were standing, Baptiste gathered deadwood to build a fire, and while part of it was burning down to cooking coals, he set out the cookware and the plates. For supper there was roast ham heated up again and served with canned apples.

Whatever else he was, Baptiste was a fair cook.

After it was over, Baptiste heated water to wash the dishes and William Manning said he was going to turn in. "It's been a long day," he mumbled. "I think—"

"Don't forget your canteen," Manning said. "You might get thirsty during the night."

"There's always the creek, Edward."

"Take care you don't get drowned in it," Manning said. "It would be an awful bother to have to ship you back to England in a barrel of rum. That's what they did with Lord Nelson after the Battle of Trafalgar. Did you know that, Sundance?"

"I must have missed that story," Sundance said.

"Oh, it isn't just a story. It's the absolute truth. After they shipped Nelson home and opened the barrel, the sailors drank the rum. I wonder what it tasted like?"

"You're disgusting," Alison Manning said. "Why do you have to make everything sound like a sneer?"

"Is that what I was doing, my dear?"

Sundance said, "Would you like me to leave so you can fight in private?" He started to get up.

Manning laughed. "Don't mind us, Sundance. We do this all the time. I believe in honesty and so does my wife. She's one of these emancipated women everyone is talking about. Free speech. Free love. They talk a lot about free love. Oh Lord! Now she's looking daggers at me, so I think I'll go to bed. See you all bright and early."

The wind was turning cold and Alison Manning huddled close to the fire with a blanket drawn about her shoulders. Baptiste had gone to sleep outside Manning's tent. In the other tent William Manning was snoring, sometimes talking in his sleep.

"Why don't you get some sleep?" Sundance said

after neither of them had spoken for five minutes.

"Don't tell me I'm tired," Alison Manning said. "I know I'm tired, but I don't feel like sleeping. What do you do when you can't sleep?"

"I always sleep," Sundance said.

"Good for you. A sound mind in a healthy body, is that it?"

"Peace, Mrs. Manning. I'm not the hero or the villain of this hunt. I'm just a hired hand."

"Don't be so modest. I know who you are and what you've done. So don't try that 'hired hand' business with me. You think we're a lot of fools, don't you?"

"That I do," Sundance agreed. "But I've been paid to do a job, and I'll do it. How you want to spend your money is none of my business. And while we're at it, my business is none of yours. Is that plain enough for you?"

Her face, already reddened by the heat of the fire, because more flushed. They were huddled by a campfire in western Colorado, but she couldn't forget she was an English lady talking to a halfbreed.

"I don't like your manner, Mr. Sundance."

"I don't like yours, Mrs. Manning."

"I could get my husband to kick you out of here."

Sundance smiled at the idea of being kicked by anyone. "No," he said. "But maybe you could get him to cancel our agreement. That wouldn't be so bad. I'd be a thousand dollars ahead."

"Then I won't ask him." She paused. "Anyway, he wouldn't do it. My husband likes you. He talks to you more than he talks to me."

"Just hunting talk. No more."

Alison Manning stared into the fire. "Has he ever said anything about me?"

"Not a word."

"Are you sure?"

"I'm sure."

"If he had said something, would you tell me?"

"No," Sundance said. "What I will tell you is this. I didn't come on this trip to be a sounding board. Not for your husband, not for you. If you don't feel like talking after this, that's fine with me."

"Go to hell, Mr. Sundance," Alison Manning said.

A spoiled bitch, Sundance thought as he built up the fire for the night. But a bitch you couldn't help liking.

In the morning, just before first light, Sundance had just finished bathing in the icy creek when Manning came down the slope and plunged in, lathering himself with harsh yellow soap. Gritting his teeth against the early morning cold, he got out of the creek and toweled himself dry.

"I hate it but I do it," he said, going through a set of exercises without effort. "Pain is good for a man, don't you think?"

"Hot coffee is better," Sundance said, pulling on his shirt.

"Where did you get all those scars?" Manning wanted to know. "Don't tell me you got all of them in battle?"

"I got them when I was initiated into Cheyenne manhood," Sundance said. "That was many years ago. I doubt that I'd do it now."

Manning finished another set of exercises and got dressed. "You did it then so you don't have to do it now. Some of the East African tribes have a similar ritual, though perhaps not so painful. I was about to bribe my way into taking part in the ceremony when the district commissioner heard about it and threatened to have me expelled from the country."

"I'm hungry," Sundance said, walking away while Manning was still lacing up his boots. Without a doubt, Edward Manning was one of the strangest men he had ever met. In his time he had met other men, just a few, who suffered from what old cavalrymen called Custeritis, meaning that bravery and cowardice was all they talked about, except that with Manning it was a serious disease rather than a minor ailment. Some day, if he didn't get over it, it would lay him in his grave.

Baptiste dished up fried ham, biscuits and coffee. After a while Manning came into camp whistling and rubbing his hands together. "Top o' the mornin'," he shouted. "That's what my old Irish grandmother used to say."

Alison Manning looked up from her plate. "Your Irish grandmother was Lady Kilcoyne and she never talked like that."

"Thank you, Baptiste," Manning said, taking a plate from the half-breed. "Maybe my Irish grandmother never said that, but there was a lot of fire in those old bones. Where do you think I got my wild blood from?"

Holding his cup with unsteady hands, William Manning said, "I don't feel a bit wild this morning. Would you mind not yelling so much, Edward?"

"You mean yelling like this?" Manning yelled so long and loud that the horses became frightened. "Or was it yelling like this?"

"That was very nice, Edward," his wife said.

"Well, I think so," Manning said, attacking his fried ham as if it were the enemy. "I think I'm going to apply to become an honorary Wild Indian before I leave here.

You think I should, Sundance?"

"I have no say in it," Sundance said. "I'm only half Indian."

"Yes, of course you are, but what does that half think?"

"It thinks you make too much noise," Sundance said. "So does the white half."

Manning slapped his knee. "Two against one. I'm outvoted. Come on now. Eat up so we can get this circus on the road."

"A menagerie is more like it," his wife said.

In an hour, after climbing a long ridge, the mountains looked a lot closer. Instead of being vague shapes in the distance, now they had depth and perspective, as if seen through a stereo viewer. On the high peaks there was snow all year; at night the wind would be cold. They saw some small game, nothing worth shooting. Manning continued in high spirits, telling Sundance stories of his years in India. There was nothing like the Indian tiger for sheer ferocity, he said. "I once shot a maneater after the old bitch had carried off nine natives from a village. Once they get the taste of human flesh, they never want to eat anything else. Hard luck for the natives when that happens. This particular village, in Bengal it was, built barricades of thorn and kept fires burning all night. Did that stop old lady tiger? Not on your life. She broke through, selected what she wanted—the last victim was a young girl—and made off with it. I got old lady tiger, but it took me a week. Staking out goats, the usual thing, was no good, so I had to wait until somebody died. The natives didn't want to give me the body until I said I'd pack up and leave if they didn't."

There were other stories about hunts in other parts of the world. It seemed that Manning had been everywhere. "I once shot a snow lion in Nepal," he said. "That's against the law up there and they wanted to cut off my head. It took the Viceroy of India to get me out of that. Did you know that there is a man in Brazil who hunts jaguars with a spear?"

The stories went on and on, but Sundance didn't mind. Oddly enough, there was no boasting in Manning's recounting of his adventures. He admitted to his failures, but then his failures had been few. Though English-born, he had no interest in England. "Napoleon was right," he said. "England *is* a nation of shopkeepers. What wouldn't I give to have lived in the days of Francis Drake, Morgan and his buccaneers. Think what it must have been like to swoop down on a Spanish galleon loaded down to the waterline with gold. What would you do if you had all that gold, Sundance? No need to answer that. You'd give it to your Indians. I might, too, come to think of it. To tell the truth, I don't know what I'd do with it. Money doesn't mean much to me."

"That's because you have so much of it," Sundance said.

Manning smiled. "You aren't thinking that I should make a contribution to your cause?"

Sundance said no. "I find the money when I need it."

"But you wouldn't turn me down if I offered you some money?"

"I'd be a fool if I did."

"Then, by God, that's what I'm going to do after this hunt is over. I haven't decided yet, but it won't be a small amount. Even if something should happen to you I'll see that the money gets to your lawyers in Washington."

"Nothing's going to happen to me," Sundance said.

"You'll be the one facing the grizzlies."

"That's true," Manning said. "But you never know what's going to happen on a hunt."

They would have reached the mountains an hour earlier if one of the pack ponies hadn't been frightened by a harmless snake. It took the better part of an hour to get the pony out of a deep draw and repack the scattered load. But nothing else happened during the day. So far the traveling had been easy. That night, after they made camp, Baptiste reported that the last of the cooked meat had turned wormy, which meant that supper would be fried bacon. It was colder that night, now that they had left the lowlands.

In the morning they moved on, climbing higher into the mountains, following a pass that looked as if no one had ever been through it. The coyotes, still howling at first light, faded away as the sun came out, washing the mountains in red. Then the red faded too, and it started to get hot.

Starting out, Manning asked, "How soon?"

Sundance knew he meant grizzlies. "Not before tomorrow. Maybe the day after. Used to be you'd find them in the foothills. Remember, you don't track grizzlies. Mostly you just come across them. Tomorrow you'd best break out the rifles."

At breakfast the next morning, Manning's wife complained about the salt bacon.

"I can have Baptiste boil some of the salt out," Manning said to annoy her even more.

That day Sundance shot a small mule deer and butchered it. Meat so fresh was inclined to be tough, but Baptiste pounded it between two smooth rocks before he put it on to cook. Everybody ate well except William Manning, who continued to drink all through the day. Never completely drunk, he said very little as the hours passed. Now and then his brother said something about his drinking, yet he did nothing to stop him. This had been going on for years, Sundance figured. There was a lot more going on than showed on the surface. What he couldn't understand was why William Manning took the riding his brother gave him. Money might have something to do with it, yet he didn't think so. Hell, he decided, why even think about it? Eleven days from now he'd be done with them for good.

The next day they saw a mountain lion, but it was gone before they even got close. Toward afternoon the pass flattened out and became a plateau that ran away for several miles. Then the mountain rose up again, stretching from north to south like a blank wall that could never be breached, and it wasn't until they reached the end of the plateau that they saw the great gaps in the mountains that would take them up to the high country that led to the peaks.

"In there," Sundance said, pointing. "That's where you'll find what you're after. There won't be many, but they're in there."

"Good," Manning said. "Now I'll show you what I'm going to shoot with."

"Isn't it a beauty?" Manning said when Baptiste brought the .300 caliber Weatherby. "I don't want to take away from your Remington, but this is the better gun. It's absolutely the best rifle made up till this time. I've had it only a few months and wonder how I could have done without it all these years. Take it, man. See for yourself."

Sundance started by bringing the Weatherby to his

shoulder in a smooth easy swing. Manning was right. It was a beautiful rifle, and like all good rifles it seemed to have a natural point. The action was smooth and precise, with little tolerance in the machined parts. It was better than the Remington. The Remington was an old and trusted friend. This rifle was better in every way.

"It's so new that very few are available," Manning said with quiet pride. "At the moment I don't think there are more than one hundred on the market. You like it?"

"Very much," Sundance said. "I'll give you the other thousand for it."

"I knew you were going to say something like that." Manning took back the rifle. "Sorry, old man, but it's not for sale. You'll get your chance when the factory goes into limited production. They'll never mass produce this work of art. But I promise you this. You will get a chance to shoot it."

CHAPTER FOUR

They climbed higher into the mountains and by the next day they were well beyond farms or settlements of any kind. It was hot by day, biting cold at night. Just before dawn Sundance heard the sound of breaking glass and he found Edward Manning digging into the packs for what was left of his brother's whiskey. One by one, he broke the quart bottles against a rock. William Manning came staggering from his tent red-eyed and cursing, but the last bottle broke before he even got close.

"You son of a bitch," William Manning yelled, grabbing a bottle with a trickle of liquor left in it. "You know I need a drink."

"Time you sobered up," Edward Manning said. "This trip is going to make a man of you. That is, if you ever were one. Now get cleaned up and eat your breakfast."

William Manning drank the dribble of whiskey and threw the bottle away. "You could have left me a decent drink. My head hurts like hell."

"How did you expect it to feel? You've had your binge and now it's over. Done with. It's too far to go back. Anyway, I wouldn't let you."

William Manning stared at the broken bottles and licked his lips. "You carry any liquor?" he asked

47

Sundance. "I'll give you ten times what it's worth."

"I don't drink," Sundance said.

William Manning walked away and Sundance said, "He's got the shakes pretty bad."

"So I see. You think I should have found an easier way to do it?"

"Tapering off is one way. It works for some men."

"It wouldn't work for William," Manning said. "I suppose William is what some people call a good man, which often means that he's simply weak. Well, for now he's going to be strong whether he likes it or not."

"He's your brother," Sundance said.

Baptiste had the fire going and William Manning sat beside it holding a cup of coffee with trembling hands.

"Load it up with sugar," Sundance said. "That'll kill some of the craving."

Alison Manning came out of her tent and looked at her husband. "What was all that noise about?" she asked.

"William decided to take the pledge," Manning said. "I helped him to decide. For his own good, of course. Don't you think he looks better?"

William Manning drank the rest of his coffee. "Look, the whiskey's gone. There's no need to make jokes about it."

"Just trying to cheer you up, old man." Manning held up a forkful of fried ham and some of the grease ran off it. "What you need is some of this. Lines the stomach and so on."

William Manning lurched to his feet and went behind his tent, where he was violently sick. Then he walked away, drinking water from a canteen.

Edward Manning smiled. "I think he's going to be all right."

"For God's sake, will you drop it?" his wife said.

"I'd much rather talk about grizzly bears, my dear."

"We're coming close to where they are," Sundance said. "Will anyone be shooting besides you?"

"My brother certainly won't. Not today anyway. My wife can shoot but doesn't really like it. So it looks like just the two of us. You still want to try the Weatherby?"

"Sure," Sundance said. "Any time you say."

William Manning came back and poured coffee without a word. He had changed into a clean shirt and washed his face and the tremor in his hands wasn't as bad as it had been.

"You're right about the sugar," he said to Sundance. "It does seem to help."

By midmorning they were five miles deeper into the mountains. Stands of pines dotted the slopes and small game was more plentiful than it had been. A whisker-faced bobcat ran away from them and disappeared in the brush.

They were making their way up a long rocky slope when the first of the grizzlies appeared without warning. It came roaring out from cover, one of the biggest bears Sundance had seen in his life, a young male with a streak of white running between its stubby ears. Sundance and Manning were in the lead. The grizzly was already charging down the slope when the second bear showed itself in snarling fury. Manning raised the Weatherby to his shoulder in a leisurely swing, aimed at the first bear and brought it crashing down with a bullet in the heart. He bolted another cartridge but held his fire. The second bear was halfway down the slope when he glanced at Sundance with a mad smile on his face. Behind them Alison Manning screamed. In another few seconds the bear would be ripping them apart.

Sundance raised the Remington. "My shot," Manning yelled and brought the second bear down no more than thirty yards away.

Fighting the urge to smash Manning in the face with the butt of his rifle, Sundance said, "Why the hell didn't you shoot? If you missed the second one some of us could be dead."

Manning ejected the spent shell from his rifle. "But I didn't miss. There was no real danger. Let me ask you something. You could have fired. Why didn't you?"

"It's your hunt," Sundance said. "Next time I won't hold back."

Manning smiled. "Now, now, don't be angry. Next time I'll shoot by the rule book. But I've learned something important about you today."

"What's that?"

"That you don't panic."

"Did you think I would?"

"No. But I wanted to be sure. Now I am."

"You scared the hell out of your wife."

"She'll get over it. Alison is used to my little surprises. Magnificent brutes, aren't they? Come on, old man. Let's get some coffee going while Baptiste attends to the trophies. You think we'll run into any more today?"

"Probably not. The shooting will send them to higher ground. They attack if they're close, but they don't go out of their way to do it. You got a pair. Not many men have done that."

"Have you?" Manning asked while the coffee boiled.

"No," Sundance said. "But I haven't hunted all that much."

"Meaning you haven't hunted that many animals. I

suppose hunting animals after you've hunted men isn't that exciting."

"To me it's just a job."

Manning said, "I once killed three men in East Africa. But there was nothing very exciting in that. They were just natives, cattle thieves armed with old muskets. Two were boys, the other an old man. They had been raiding a farm owned by a friend of mine. He asked me to help."

Baptiste worked expertly on the male grizzly, peeling off the hide, taking great care with the head.

"Have you eaten bear meat?" Manning asked.

"Now and then. It's all right if you can't get anything else."

"I think a man should do everything," Manning said. "So that when the end of his life comes he knows he hasn't missed anything."

Alison Manning had been scratching in the dirt with a stick. She now broke it in two and tossed it into the fire. "The world is too tame for my husband," she said. "The army was too tame, so he resigned. Even at school he went out for all the strenuous sports. He boxed, wrestled, climbed mountains. You can't possibly be as brave as my husband, Mr. Sundance."

"I'll manage," Sundance said.

"Perhaps you think you're braver but don't want to say so?"

William Manning poured coffee and once again loaded it with sugar. Finally he spoke to his brother, urging him to give up the hunt so they could go back to Trinidad.

"You got two big ones," he said. "What more do you want?"

"I know what you want," Manning said. "You're

not sober half a day and you're dreaming of whiskey. So the answer is no. We're going on with the hunt. Just drink your sickening coffee. I don't want to hear any more about it.''

For a moment William Manning seemed ready to talk back, to assert his right as a man to go where he pleased. But the moment passed and William Manning knew that he wasn't going to do anything. Alison Manning looked away from him, not wanting to meet his stricken eyes. Sundance wondered if there was something between the brothers that the woman didn't know about. There had to be something to keep William Manning so submissive, for he didn't have the look of a born coward.

Baptiste treated the bearskins and laid them out, wet side up, to catch a few hours of sun before he packed them on the ponies. There was nothing to do but wait around and let the day drag on.

In the afternoon William Manning took his rifle and started away from camp.

''Where are you going?'' his brother said.

''To shoot something.''

''Not yourself, I hope.''

William Manning went on without answering. About an hour later a single shot echoed in the hills. They all stopped what they were doing and listened for another. There was none. Sometime later William Manning came back with a small pronghorn slung over his shoulders. He dumped the carcass by the fire and said, ''One shot at three hundred yards. This is something we can eat.''

''It's no grizzly bear,'' his brother said.

They got in a few hours travel before darkness started to close in. It got very cold after the sun dropped below the horizon and the ground gave up the day's heat. That night, for the first time since they started from

Trinidad, William Manning ate well for the first time. To Sundance it seemed like the man was trying to get hold of himself. A spark of defiance was beginning to show itself at last. No one talked very much until William Manning announced that he was going to turn in.

"Wait," Edward Manning said. "Perhaps I've been a bit too hard on you."

"I don't care what you think about it."

"What I mean is, I didn't break every bottle. There's one left. One bottle can't do you that much harm, can it? Baptiste, get the bottle for my brother."

When Manning got the bottle he spun it and caught it just before it hit the ground. "You want a drink?" he asked.

William Manning caught the bottle when it was thrown to him. Then his eyes darted around the campfire, fixing each of them in turn.

"Sleep tight, brother," Manning said.

Baptiste grunted. It might have been a laugh.

Without warning, William Manning shattered the bottle against a rock and waited for his brother's reaction.

"You'll probably regret that," he said. "In the dark hours when you wake up, you'll wish you hadn't done that."

"We'll see," William Manning said. "Yesterday I would have. Today is different."

Manning yawned. "Brave words, old man. Now if our little drama has concluded, I think I'll turn in myself."

They had camped high up, and when morning came

they could see far across the mountains, bare and brown in the strong sunlight. Breakfast was over and Edward Manning was whistling while they took down the tents. After the work was done he straightened up and pointed.

"Is that the badlands? What you call the Four Corners?"

Sundance nodded. "We better go easy on the water after this. That's hard country in there."

Manning smiled confidently. "Then this is just the place to start."

"Start what?"

"The real hunt. Don't turn. Baptiste has his rifle pointed at your spine." Manning drew the big Webley pistol from its holster and cocked it. "It fires double-action, but that can throw off the aim, not that there's much chance of missing at this distance. Stay where you are, my dear. You too, William. No talking please. Take his weapons, Baptiste."

Sundance did nothing while the half-breed took his pistol, hatchet and knife. There was nothing to do, not right now. The whole thing had been a pretext from the very beginning, and now he knew why the Englishman hadn't picked another guide.

"Look for a knife strapped to his leg," Manning ordered. "I think you'll find one. There you see. That's what I call defanging the snake. You aren't saying anything, Sundance?"

"What's the play?" Sundance said. Even if the half-breed hadn't been behind him, there was no chance against a cocked .455 in the hands of a dead shot.

"Sit on that rock," Manning ordered. "Sit and listen to the rules. In a way this is the highest compliment I can pay you. I wanted to hunt the most dangerous man I could find. That's you, old man. From the beginning there was no other choice. Doesn't that please you?"

"Not much." From where he was Sundance could see Manning's wife and brother. The woman's face was white and she was trembling. William Manning sat holding a coffee cup. Baptiste had moved back and was holding the rifle at his hip.

"Like it or not, you're elected," Manning said. "I'm surprised you didn't catch on before now. I gave you plenty of hints."

"I didn't think you were crazy, Manning."

The Englishman waved his free hand, but kept the revolver steady. "I'm not a bit crazy. I'm just doing what I want to do. I always have. That's the difference between me and other men."

"But there's more?" Sundance said, knowing there was.

"Well, yes, there is. There's my wife and her lover, my dear brother. She came to him for sympathy during my long absences and he gave it to her. Of course she didn't know I knew, but he did because I told him. How do you think I got him to come along on this hunt?"

Sundance glanced over at the wife and brother. "By threatening to kill her. Something like that."

"Exactly like that," Manning said. "I made a bargain with William. Come along with me while I hunt you. If you kill me, then my dear brother gets to inherit the little woman and all my worldly goods."

"What happens if I don't kill you?"

"Then I'll kill my wife and brother. It's a bit complicated, I admit, but I couldn't very well hunt my brother. He's not up to it, never was. So I had to give him odds. You're the odds, Sundance."

"They'll ask questions in Trinidad if you come back

short three people. The marshal there is a good man. He'll want to know what happened."

"Bandits. Outlaws. Brigands." Manning laughed, pleased at his own cleverness. "You can blame anything on bandits. One bullet is like another. Ballistics is a new science. They won't have it here. You know what I think? I think you think I'm ready to go back on my bargain. No such thing. You kill me and the lovebirds go free."

"What about Baptiste?"

Manning laughed again. "I think it's probably better if you kill him too. He has his instructions, but he's very loyal to me. Anything else you'd like to know?"

Sundance knew that nothing he said would change the Englishman's mind. He had the arrogance of someone born to money and the utter confidence of a man who knew how to kill. More than that, he was sure he could get away with it. In this country, maybe he could.

"Do I get a weapon?" Sundance asked.

"The bowie knife," Manning said. "I've been told you're good with it. The knife and a canteen of water and some matches. I want to give you a chance, but I don't want to give you too much of a chance. On the other hand, you have the advantage of knowing this country."

Sundance was thinking about Eagle. "What about my horse?"

"You don't get the horse."

"That's not what I meant. If you're planning to kill my horse you'd better kill me first. I won't run for you if you kill my horse. You make the choice right now."

Sundance stood up and took a step toward the cocked Webley. Manning didn't move and the pistol didn't waiver. "Nobody's going to kill your horse. It will be

56

turned loose and driven back the other way. Is that good enough for you?''

"It'll do.''

"You'll get an hour's start," Manning said. "You better go now before my dear wife bursts into tears. It's too bad you didn't get a chance to shoot my Weatherby. Come to think of it, perhaps you will.''

"I'll try hard to do that," Sundance said.

All that day Sundance ran, and now with the failed ambush behind him he was running again. Manning had outguessed him and was coming after him another way. He kept to solid rock as much as possible, hoping to gain time by throwing the hunter off his trail. But he knew Manning would pick it up and keep following. He wondered about a night ambush, but decided to try it only as a last resort.

He took a sip of water and ran fast across a meadow bright with flowers. There was a long open stretch to be crossed and he waited for the bullet that might come at any moment. He had gone for more than a day without food, but for now water was more important.

He guessed that Manning was far ahead of the others by now, with Baptiste pushing the wife and brother on at the point of a gun. William Manning could shoot, but he was no match in ferocity for the half-breed. He didn't belong in this country. Neither did the woman. Looking for help in that direction was a waste of time.

Staying off the ridges as much as he could, Sundance chewed on a handful of berries while he ran. It started to get dark and that lessened the chances of a shot even with the scoped Weatherby. Manning might come in the dark, taking the chance of being ambushed, but there was nothing to do but lie up in cover and get some sleep. He had been running for a day and a half and the lack of food was beginning to drain his strength.

A late spring shower woke him in almost total darkness and he snatched off his hat and tried to catch some water before the sky cleared. Naked except for pants and moccasins, he shivered as the cold night rain beat down on him. After the rain stopped there was enough water in the hat to halt his thirst. A young moon came out, lighting the mountains with feeble light. Before he moved on he pulled out several thorns that had begun to fester. It rained again, just a wind-driven shower that drifted over the mountains and away to the south, leaving nothing to drink. Without a shirt or coat he was cold in the wind that followed the rain, but he steeled his mind against feeling it.

At first light, resting again after traveling through the long hours of darkness, he raised his head when he saw a black-tailed jackrabbit hopping through the brush about fifteen feet beyond him. The animal, sensing danger, raised its head and sniffed at the sky. Sundance held his breath and didn't move as the rabbit came out of the brush to nibble at a patch of berries. It raised its head and sniffed again, then went on eating. Sundance edged the bowie knife from its scabbard and lined up the distance he had to throw. If he missed there wouldn't be another chance. Worse than missing was the thought that the wounded animal might drag the knife down in a deep hole.

He hurled the knife without getting up. The heavy blade flashed in the dull morning light and the jack rabbit screamed, jumped into the air, and fell dead. There was no need to run, but he ran, thinking of the knife, his one chance of coming out of this. The rabbit was still quivering when he pulled out the knife and cut the animal's throat. Feeling no revulsion—nothing—he drank the hot, spurting blood. Then he sat down heavily and skinned the carcass. He separated the fatty hindquarters and cut them into thin slices. Eating the raw meat was something he had to do. It tasted rank but it was food. The sun was showing red by the time he finished.

When there was nothing left to eat, he licked the blood off his hands. Another day of hell lay ahead of him, but there was food in his belly and he was still alive.

For what it's worth, Sundance thought.

CHAPTER FIVE

That day twenty-five or thirty wild burros broke from the cover of a deep draw and ran away in front of him, braying and kicking up their heels. He followed their tracks for a while, then cut away from them, not sure that Manning wouldn't outguess him again. But making a choice wouldn't be easy for the hunter. If he stayed with the herd he would be led miles out of his way. Anything was worth a try.

Sundance began to think about making a bow. His weapons belt was made from braided rawhide. It wasn't the best thing to use to string a bow but it was all he had. What he needed for the bow was ash. The arrows would be made from the same wood, or something harder if he could find it.

Crossing another mountain meadow he found a stand of ash. Watching the meadow behind him, he chose an ash branch with the right amount of spring in it. He cut it and trimmed it, the easiest part of the job. Nothing showed on the wide meadow as he looked up now and then. He knew Manning wouldn't be able to see him in the shade of the trees. But there was no guarantee that Manning, even armed with the rifle, would start across a long, exposed stretch of ground.

He unbraided the weapons belt, leaving just enough

to support the bowie knife and sheath. Then he notched the ends of the bow so the twisted and rejoined rawhide could be tied securely. When he tested the bow there was too much play and not enough tension. He had to string it again. By the time the wood began to dry, there would be enough force to make a decent shot.

Cutting the arrows took more time. There was nothing to use for arrowheads. All he could do was sharpen the heads to short points that wouldn't break off too easily. He fashioned three arrows, then notched the ends and pushed in pieces of flat bark to function as feathers. An hour after he started he was finishing up when he saw the flash of a rifle barrel on the other side of the meadow.

It came up out of the waving grass and then Manning came after it. Then nothing else happened. There was no chance here, Sundance knew, so he went on, getting out of the trees without being seen. It would have to be a place where Manning wouldn't be so careful. And it might not work at all no matter where he tried it. If the makeshift arrow hit a bone or stuck in Manning's canvas coat, he'd find himself too close to the rifle. The stomach was the spot to try for, or the gut right below the belt. If he could drive an arrow deep enough, Manning would die anyway, and once he had the Weatherby he could pick off Baptiste at any distance he liked.

If he got the chance.

He wondered how Manning was holding up after two days of hard travel. It was hard to say, and it could even be that Manning had prepared for this hunt in the badlands of some other country. Maybe there had been weeks of driving himself, running, sweating, going without water until all the fat was boiled out of him and only muscle remained. But there was one flaw that Manning hadn't considered for all his preparations, all his worked-out plans. Any man could be killed and not always by someone with more nerve and better weapons. John Wesley Harding, the deadliest killer who ever lived, had been dropped with a bullet in the back of the head. Hickok was dead too, blasted into hell by a drunken little coward who wanted to be famous. Sundance smiled sourly. But he hadn't done the blasting with an arrow that might not shoot straight.

Late that day, with no sign of Manning, Sundance used one of the arrows on a jack rabbit. It worked all right and the rabbit died. He drank the rabbit's blood and carried the still dripping carcass, waiting for darkness before he ate the meat.

That night he made his way through a deep valley with rock walls, and when he climbed up out of it there was a mesa with more mountains jutting up from the end of it. Up so high there was fog and it was cold. The mesa was brown with moss on the rocks. A bleak place that provided little cover, but after he crossed the flattest part there were low ridges again. By the time he put the ridges behind him, he knew he was coming down to flatland that was the center of the Four Corners. Down there were sand dunes, long waves of blinding white gypsum sand.

He crossed a dried-up creek that would run with wild flash floods when it rained. Now there wasn't even a trace of water. He crossed the creek and rested in the shade of the cottonwoods that grew along its banks. He allowed himself an hour's sleep, and during those sixty minutes he dreamed of hot coffee and frying steak.

By morning he reached the sand dunes, rolling on ahead of him like a white sea. Organ pipe cactus, green and spiky, looked black against the glare of the dunes. The sun grew fierce before seven o'clock and far off buzzards wheeled in the sky. He tested the bow and the wood was drying fast, stretching the rawhide until it twanged under his finger.

The dunes ran away for miles, then there was a stretch of alkali beds. The bitter dust stung his eyes and he wrapped his bandanna around his mouth and nose to keep from choking. At noon the sun was directly overhead and seemed to stay there for a long time. Beyond the alkali flats were black lava beds and then the sand dunes started again. In places he was knee-deep in sand and when he got over the crest of a dune he had to fight to keep from falling.

Though he only sipped at the water, the last of it was gone by late afternoon. He held the canteen high until the final drop fell into his mouth. Even so, the sun wasn't so bad now. The mountains looked closer. He looked back. There was no sign of Manning. Either he was hanging back or the desert was wearing him down. Somehow, Sundance didn't think so.

Sitting in the shadow of a giant cactus, Sundance watched the slope of a dune about five hundred yards from where he was. In the bright moonlight the sand looked like snow. Here he would wait for Manning, for there were no tracks in the sand to show where he had gone. If Manning came before morning, he would wait in the shadows and try for a shot. With the big rifle in his hands, he could go looking for Baptiste.

The night wind blowing across the tops of the dunes had a ghostly sound. Under the cold moon the powdery sand looked like a high drift after a snowfall. The night was alive with the sounds of small night creatures. A sidewinder swam through the sand, hunting for rodents.

It looped and twisted its way into the shadows and disappeared.

Sundance dug the bowie into the cactus, then turned it until he could pull out a chunk. It was bitter tasting, but there was some moisture in it. He wondered how Alison Manning was taking this strange journey so far from damp, green England. People made their own hells, he guessed, or at least they helped others to make them on their behalf. She had started out with a brute and ended up with—what was William Manning?

He stopped thinking about William Manning when he saw something move at the top of the dune. But it was just a coyote and it was dragging some small animal. When the moon began to pale, he knew it was time to start again. Keeping to the shadows of the giant cactuses, he was soon too far away even for the Weatherby. After six hundred yards he knew he was out of range.

The desert began to peter out by morning. The sand gave way to broken ground that sloped up toward the mountains. In a while the air was cooler and the sky seemed to lose the pitiless look it had in the desert. There wasn't a sound except for the wind.

Suddenly it came to him that Manning wasn't going to try for any long-distance shooting. What the hunter wanted to do was drive him to the breaking point, to watch him crawl from hunger and thirst and exhaustion. That was it. That's what it had been all along. Manning didn't just want to kill him. He wanted to break his spirit, to make him beg. Manning had finally found the sport he liked better than any other. He couldn't just settle for a merciful bullet. Manning had said that this hunt was his last, but at the time he was talking about animals. Now that he had discovered the thing he always craved behind the English good manners, he would go on killing. Maybe not always like this, but he would find other ways.

Lying behind a cleft rock, Sundance saw Manning come up out of the desert. At first his figure was blurred by the heat waves that shimmered over the sand. But it firmed up as he came ahead, not fast but with purpose, holding the rifle at the ready. Sundance squinted against the glare of the sun, and even if he had been armed with a rifle, the range was too great. Manning was at least four hundred yards away, maybe more. In the clear desert air distances were deceiving even to the most experienced eye.

Sundance moved back from where he was because Manning would spot the cleft rock before long. At last Manning was showing himself in the open by daylight. That didn't mean that he had become reckless or impatient. It could be a change of strategy, or just part of a plan that he had worked out long before.

So far Sundance had done all the running, keeping ahead of the Englishman as best he could. Now he was going to change his own tactics, moving from one likely place of ambush to another. He would pick good places and then abandon them, always moving back, but never too far. Manning would follow, picking up his trail and moving on again. Then, sometime during the day, he would choose a place of ambush and stay with it. It would not be the best place he could find, or too obviously the worst, but something in between. There he would try for a kill or a wound that would bring Manning down long enough so he could be finished off with the knife.

If Manning didn't outguess him again.

Here there were rocks as big as houses, piled one on top of the other. No brush, just rocks and sand and the open spaces that divided them. At no time did he show himself, not because of the scoped rifle, but because it would have been too obvious. He was letting the Englishman get closer than he had been at any time since the hunt began. If Manning moved fast he might be able to get ahead of him. That would be the end of it.

Now and then he made an attempt to cover his tracks, knowing that Manning would find them easily enough. He was very tired, so Manning had to be just as tired, probably more so. Manning's life in wild places might have hardened him, yet all the things he had done were of his own choosing. There had been few times in Manning's life when he couldn't have backed off and gone home, whereas the hardships Sundance endured were dictated by necessity. All that might make some difference. Sundance hoped it would.

Hours passed as they played the game of advance and retreat. There were times when he could see Manning. When that happened he dropped out of sight, increasing the distance so that Manning was always in back of him. There was a long stretch of time when Manning didn't seem to be moving at all. Then after climbing to a high rock, flat on his belly and sweating, Sundance saw a kangaroo rat run twittering into the open and he knew the rodent hadn't been disturbed by a snake because snakes didn't hunt by day. It had to be Manning.

He inched forward on the rock but couldn't see anything. It looked like Manning had holed up under a shelf of rock that threw a long shadow. Sundance smiled grimly. They had been playing advance and retreat; now Manning was trying to get him to do some advancing himself. There was only one thing wrong with Manning's position: it was too easily defended, and that made it hard to get out of without being seen.

Sundance eased down from the rock and moved closer to Manning's position, keeping to cover, and when he was close enough he found his own rock-thrown shadow where the sun didn't reach. Manning made no sounds; he was too clever a manhunter to try that. But he was there all right. Sundance knew that by watching the kangaroo rat. Time after time it came back to where it lived, only to skitter away at the last moment.

When it got dark Sundance moved a little closer to make sure that Manning wouldn't elude him when the light got bad. If he came out now he had a chance if the moon stayed down. But it didn't and soon it cast a cold light so strong that even the scope might be used with a fair chance of success.

Nothing happened for hours. The moon had faded and the sky was a deep velvet blue with stars set in it. It was cold and quiet and with many hours to go till morning. Sundance didn't raise his head as a flare exploded silently in the sky far back over the desert. The flare went up high and burst apart. It hung there, suspended, a blue and white ball of light brighter than the stars. Still dripping light, it began to fall, and when there was no light from the first flare a second flare went up a few minutes later.

A third flare went up and Sundance moved forward. As soon as he did a bullet from the Weatherby came close to his head. He threw himself flat as bullets sang all around him. Manning was firing for effect now, pinning Sundance down so he himself could get out. Every time the bolt slammed back and forward a bullet came at him. They came fast. The flare could be a distress signal or a trick to draw him out. But then he heard boots thudding in the sand and he knew that Manning had broken out of his position and was going back toward the desert. That, too, could be part of a plan. He stayed where he was.

He waited.

Darkness glimmered to light and he knew Manning wasn't there any more. He watched the kangaroo rat coming back to the shelf of rock. Later he saw Manning's boot marks in the sand that went back toward the place where the desert began. He stopped when he came to a stretch of sand and saw that the boot marks went all the way to the other side. Another trap? Maybe. He turned back.

Again he climbed high and watched while the sun crossed the sky. Nothing stirred in the desolation of sand and rock that lay below his vantage point. He gave it thirty minutes and decided there was no sure answer to what the flares meant. If he started now he could lose his tracks and try to make his way over the mountains to New Mexico. The water was gone but he thought he could make it. There had to be water—some water somewhere—but even as he thought about it, he knew he couldn't leave this business unfinished, and it wasn't just because Manning had hunted him. There were men —a few—still alive that Sundance hated and would kill, if given the opportunity, yet he wasn't prepared to follow them to the ends of the earth. Edward Manning was different in that he would grow worse if left alive. If the man he wanted most to kill went free, then he would kill other men as a way of making up for it.

Sundance climbed high again but there was nothing to see. If Manning had gone back into the desert, and not just pretended to, it had to be for a good reason. Something had gone wrong.

That Manning would follow him again Sundance had no doubt. After all, there was the law—such as it was—to be considered. What Manning had done, or tried to do, would earn him a quick hanging or, at the very least, life in prison. No judge, no jury would hold still for what Manning had done. In the West men killed for many and sometimes trifling reasons, but Manning's reasons were so peculiar that no one would understand or even be prepared to.

In the afternoon the wind blew hard and dusty, not enough to be called a duststorm, but enough to make Sundance take refuge, to wait until it was over. By the time the wind died down all tracks were lost, his and Manning's. To draw Manning on was now his object, as it had been before. Manning and the water he carried. But for now there was nothing to do but rest up in the shade.

The edge of the bowie had been dulled by cutting the bow. He sharpened it on a piece of petrified wood, moving the blade back and forth with hardly a sound. He couldn't wet the stone because his mouth was dry. There was no cactus here, not a drop of moisture in all this wasteland. The hours passed and Manning had not returned from the desert. Manning had lost his advantage; he could have no way of knowing where Sundance was. There would be no better chance to kill the Englishman now.

An arrow in the belly was still the best bet. The arrows had been slightly warped by the sun and he straightened the still soft wood. The bowie wasn't meant for throwing, but he knew how to do it, though he had the true knife fighter's reluctance to let go of his blade. It would have to be done fast, for even a belly wound would give Manning time to draw the Webley. If he didn't move swiftly he would be running into six bullets.

He was still bending the arrows when he saw Manning again. The others were about half a mile behind. Too far away to see clearly, it looked like Baptiste was supporting William Manning as he walked. Manning's wife was with them, walking dejectedly by herself. Manning got closer, advancing warily with the rifle in both hands. Once he stopped and looked up at the rocks, but not at where Sundance was. Then he moved ahead again, holding the rifle across his chest. His canvas coat was open.

Sundance sprang from cover and loosed the arrow. Manning yelled as it buried itself high in his chest. By then Sundance was running at him with the bowie. He raised it shoulder high for the throw. Then a bullet struck the haft of the knife and tore it from his hands. Manning hadn't fired. The bullet had come from the side. As Sundance dived for cover, Manning got off one shot before bullets kicked up sand all around him and a rough voice ordered him to throw down the rifle. There was an instant of silence, then Sundance heard the clatter of the rifle as it hit the ground. Back where the others were there was a scatter of shots.

Sundance raised his head when the same rough voice told him to come out. The face that belonged to the voice was hairy and dirty under a floppy hat. A gob of tobacco juice spattered on a rock close to Sundance's head.

"Get up," the hairy man said. He was tall, gaunt and stoop-shouldered. His blue shirt was stiff with dried sweat. As he spoke his jaws worked on the chaw of

71

tobacco. He stared at Sundance. "What the hell is going on here, you mind telling me that?"

He turned to another man, a younger version of himself. "How bad is that feller hurt? Arrow get to the lung?"

"Don't look like it, Lowry. You want me to kill him?"

Lowry spat. "You are a fool, Rufus," he growled. "Course I don't want you to kill him. Why in hell do you think we went to so much trouble? And that fine rifle you're holding belongs to me. Don't damage it or I'll damage you. Get on down and hurry the others along."

There were about a dozen men with Lowry, all dirty and ragged, all heavily armed. Two of them pushed Manning forward, with the arrow still sticking in his chest. His light blue eyes were expressionless as he looked at Sundance.

"You came close," he said.

"You talk when I tell you," Lowry roared, but there was no real anger in his voice. "Now you hold still while I cut off most of that arrow. Damned if I ever seen an arrow looked like that." Lowry drew a dirk from his belt. "Hold him, boys."

"No need," Manning said.

Lowry drew a trickle of blood from Manning's throat with the needle point of the Arkansas Toothpick. "Didn't I just tell you not to talk? You don't do nothing less I tell you. Then you'll talk, sing, whistle and dance. Them's the rules."

Holding the arrow steady, Lowry cut it off about three inches from the wound. "Too high to pierce a lung," he said. "I'll get the rest of it out when we get back to camp. After that I'll decide what to do with you. Well curse me and curse my cat! We just got ourself a woman."

The man called Rufus said, "The other half-breed got killed. This feller's got something wrong with his leg. Can't hardly walk. The lady's got nothing wrong with her though." Rufus rubbed his crotch. "She's a looker all right."

"Too much talk," Lowry said. "Fetch the horses and move them out. It looks like we happened onto something good here. Take good care of my rifle, boy. It smells of money. Everything here smells of money, and believe me that's a sweeter smell than a whore's armpit."

Lowry swept off his filthy hat and held it against his chest. "Begging the lady's pardon naturally. Us pore fellers ain't used to such fine company."

"You're a card, Lowry," Rufus said, rubbing his crotch again. "Damn if that lady ain't a looker."

"Shut your poxy mouth and put them on the horses," Lowry said. "I got a lot of questions to ask when we get in the shade."

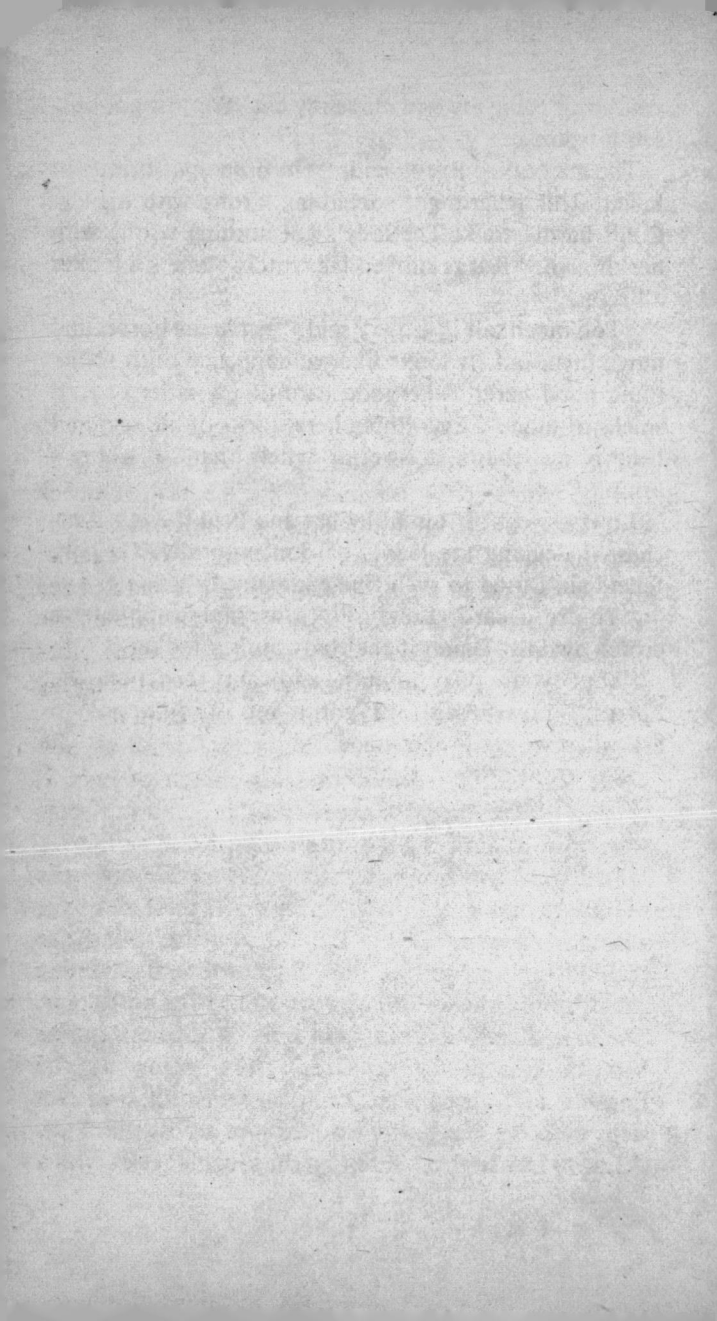

CHAPTER SIX

Mounted on a gelding that had seen better days, Lowry led the way back to camp, a deep canyon sheltered from the sun with a spring bubbling from the base of a rock wall. There was a rough stone house with one side of the roof caved in. The stones had been fitted together without mortar or mud. Sundance knew it hadn't been built by Lowry or any of his men. Without a doubt the original owner had gone to his grave or to some other part of the country. Smoketrees grew close to the spring and there was a split rail corral with horses in it.

Lowry pointed. "There's the water, drink all you want. Rufus, go see how that new batch of corn is coming along. If it's cooked, fill a jug and get some water. Lord, ain't it good to get out of that sun?"

Watched by Lowry's men, Sundance and the Mannings drank clear, cold spring water until they were gasping. As soon as his thirst had gone, Sundance realized how hungry he was. Sundance and Manning stood up together and their eyes locked for an instant. The hate surged up in Sundance like a sickness and he had to turn away to keep from going at the Englishman's throat. He knew he wouldn't take two steps before a gun barrel cracked him across the skull.

Lowry had settled himself on the sagging porch with a

jug of moonshine and a pitcher of water. Tipping whiskey into a tin cup, he roared, "You people get up there. That spring ain't about to run dry, if that's what you're thinking. Maybe I'll give you a drink if you give me the right and truthful answers to my questions. Try lying to me and you'll get something else. Rufus, fetch a chair for the lady, you unmannerly bastard. The rest of you sit any place you like."

Lowry pointed to Manning. "You got the look of a feller as orders folks around. You in charge of this peculiar party? Say your name and then say the rest of it. Some kind of foreigner, ain't you?"

"My name is Edward Manning and I'm an Englishman."

"Get on with it." Lowry tipped the jug again.

Manning told the truth, leaving nothing out. Now and then Lowry licked his tongue against his store teeth. He was close to the end of it when Lowry frowned and held up his hand.

"Rufus," he roared. "You come out here, you son of a bitch."

Rufus came out of the house with a plate of beans in his hand. "What's eating on you now, Lowry? Can't a man fill his belly in peace after a long hot ride?"

Lowry shifted the wad of tobacco to the side of his mouth while he knocked back a cup of whiskey. "Will you look at the son of a bitch! Like pig shit wouldn't melt in his mouth. First off, Rufus, you ain't a man, so don't go claiming to be one."

"That ain't nice, Lowry," Rufus complained. "Saying such a thing before strangers. Say what you want so's I can get back to my grub."

Lowry glared at him. "You're my own son, but, oh, how I hate you, boy. Here I am sitting and listening and it just came to me I ain't seen none of the wallets nor valuables these foreigners must've had on them. You ain't about to tell me they was walking around with empty pockets?''

Rufus swallowed hard. "I just forgot, Lowry. You know I wasn't about to steal from my own father. You know I wouldn't do a mean thing like that."

"Like hell. You'd steal from the dead." Lowry drank more moonshine. "So would I, but I'd share what I stole. That's the trouble with you. You ain't got no family feeling. Now go and fetch them things before I get excited and kick your hind end."

Rufus came back with wallets and watches and Alison Manning's wedding ring. "You want the guns too, Lowry?"

"Leave the goddamned guns, you fool. You sure you ain't holding something back?''

"I swear, Lowery. My grub's getting cold. All right I go back and finish it?''

Lowry waved him away and began to root through the wallets belonging to the Manning brothers. He held up a small gold plate that Sundance recognized as a railroad pass. Lowry held it so he could read the engraved writing. It took him a while.

"God bless you," he said to Manning. "You told the truth after all. 'From Colonel J.C. Dodge to the Honorable Edward Manning.' I don't know as I ever seen one of these things. You know the colonel?''

"He was a friend of my father's," Manning said.

"I knew you was money," Lowry said. "A man that knows the man that built the Union Pacific has to be important. You sure carry a lot of money. Didn't nobody warn you this country is chock full of desperadoes and men of a general bad nature?''

William Manning sat on the edge of the porch with both hands gripping his damaged knee. His face, badly burned by the sun, was set in lines of pain.

"Mr. Lowry," Edward Manning said, touching the piece of arrow still in his chest.

"Oh that," Lowry said. "That ain't in deep or you wouldn't be talking so free. We'll get her out in a minute. What happened to your brother's leg? The half-breed do that too?"

Manning said, "A cougar scared our pack ponies right off a ledge. My brother tried to stop them and went over too."

"Foolish man," Lowry said, holding up William Manning's wallet. "Something here that bothers me a little bit. How come you don't carry as much folding money as the Honorable Edward? That's your brother."

"I'm not as rich," William Manning said, grimacing with pain.

"Maybe you just have better sense? You ain't honorable too, are you?"

"Just not as rich."

Lowry said, "Why that?"

William Manning explained that in England the first-born son inherited everything. The other sons had to wait until he died.

"Not fair," Lowry said. "It's laws like that that causes men to turn to the crooked road. Was you in on this thing of hunting the breed? Don't seem to me you're the kind of a man would go with that."

"That was my brother's idea," William Manning said.

"Mr. Lowry," Edward Manning said. "Would you mind telling us what you're going to do with us?"

"What I like."

Sundance knew that Lowry was just as big a threat as Manning, and maybe more so, because the talk of killing was so casual. The name Lowry meant nothing to him. The Southwest was full of drifting bands of outlaws and killers.

"You sure talk like a tent-show actor," Lowry said. "But Colonel Dodge says you ain't, and who am I to doubt the colonel? You're fancy all right. Even your boots are fancy. Mine ain't. You'd be wearing a size eleven. Take 'em off and we'll swap."

"There's a new pair my man was carrying. The half-breed you killed."

Throwing back his head, half drunk, Lowry roared for his son Rufus to come out.

"What's it now?" Rufus said.

"You stole my new boots," Lowry roared. "You made off with my new laced boots this foreigner just give me. How in hell did you figure to wear new boots without me seeing it?"

Lowry, waiting for Rufus, pulled off his broken boots, exposing large dirty feet. Sundance wondered what Manning's wife was thinking. England must have seemed like a place she'd never see again. If that's what she thought, she was right. All Lowry had to do was kill them and let the buzzards do the rest.

"Strong but soft as glove leather," Lowry announced when he got the boots on. "Always steal the best is my motto. These boots is going to last me nigh into my old age."

Manning tried again. "Look. You're got my rifle, boots, money—everything we have. There's five thousand dollars in my wallet. You have two gold watches, the other rifles and revolvers. Don't you think you ought to let us go? What more do you want?"

"A lot," Lowry said.

"How much?"

"Would fifty thousand be asking too much?" Lowry said. "I'm not a greedy man. Don't want to leave you short. You can raise fifty thousand?"

"Yes, I can," Manning answered.

A grin spread across Lowry's hairy face. "You say that so easy. Which means you can raise twice as much. A hundred thousand. That's the price of your life."

Manning's red face grew redder. "How do you propose to get it?"

"That's up to you. You figure it out and we'll see how it goes. I just know a smart feller like you will think of how it can be done. You think as a pore man I'd carry a grudge against quality folks. No such thing. I like quality folks. When I say quality that don't mean I include the breed here. If I didn't hear the story from your own mouth I wouldn't have believed it. But like they say it's so strange it just can't be made up. You hired the breed so you could hunt him down. Naturally he didn't know that when you hired him. You turned him loose with nothing but a knife and you with that long-distance rifle. Not such good odds. Course I wouldn't give him any kind of odds, was I planning to kill him. You must think highly of the breed. I mean as an enemy."

"I didn't think of him as an enemy."

Lowry grinned again with his store teeth. "Here I'm drinking moon and you're the one is drunk. I'll say it again. You think this breed is mighty dangerous?"

Manning didn't look at Sundance. "Not so dangerous. He knows the country better than I do. I didn't want to give him too much of a chance."

"He had you dead to rights the way I saw it. Sure he did. You owe me a debt of gratitude. Say you owe me or I'll kill you."

Lowry was about sixty, but his big hands were fast. The pistol came out cocked.

Manning stared at the muzzle. "I owe you," he said.

Lowry set down the hammer and holstered the revolver. "See, you ain't so brave," he said. "You should have figured that I wouldn't kill no golden gander. You want me to kill the breed for you? No trouble. I'll go you one better. You want my pistol and one bullet so you can kill him yourself? A mark of good faith. I'm ready to give you a pistol 'cause I know you ain't going to try to shoot me. Would be riddled from belly to brisket if you did."

"I don't want it," Manning said.

"You wasn't about to get it," Lowry said.

"I don't want to kill Sundance. The trouble between us is over."

"Seems to me the trouble was all one-sided. I told you to think on a way to get my hundred thousand. That what you been doing? Before you answer, you'd better know a few things about me. I'm getting old and I ain't got no money. Was a time when me and the boys robbed and raided all over New Mexico. But the rewards kept getting bigger and the money we stole smaller. Nigh on a year ago the biggest posse you ever saw chased us into these badlands. They give up after a spell and we was heading for Colorado—hoping to get there—when we come across this old miner's place. Been here ever since. Nice place—the old dead man even had a still—but we'd like to get out. Never enough food 'cept what we can shoot. We're desperate men, is what I mean. Desperate enough to do anything. Kill. Torture. Anything. You understand now?"

"I understand," Manning said. "Do I have your word that you'll let us go when you get the money?"

Lowry jetted tobacco juice at a fly that had settled on the edge of the porch. "As a gentleman," he said. "What bothers me is your country is such a long ways off. Ain't you got money closer than that? Important feller like you's got to have rich friends this side of the water. I'd like it better if you did."

"New York," Manning said. "I had money transferred to a New York bank. The manager will telegraph a money draft to any bank I say. The cash can be picked up. That was the arrangement."

"How will this manager know it's you that's asking for the money?"

"He gave me an account number nobody else knows about. That's all that's needed."

"The wonders of the business world," Lowry said, tipping the jug again. "Cash and carry. I like that. Was afraid you was going to ask me to take a check. You did that and I'd have to light a fire under your feet. Like the sign in the barbershop: NO TRUST. Now there's only one thing left. Who's going to send the telegraph? Who's going to pick up the money? Can't be me or none of the boys. Not a one of us has the right face for the job. So who?"

Listening to Lowry, Sundance decided that the old bandit was a very shrewd man for all his folksy rambling. Some men hid their real intentions behind a screen of words. He wondered if Manning realized the kind of man he was dealing with.

"I'd be the likely one to go," Manning said. "It's my money and I can prove who I am if I have to."

"Most sensible on the face of it," Lowry said.

"You do have my wife and brother as hostages."

"Sure I do. And I have you, Englishman. I think I'd like to keep you where I can see you. You're the prize in this package."

"You think I'd try to escape and leave my family to take the consequences?" Manning looked indignant.

Lowry shrugged. "Mister, I don't know what you'd do. Who can say after what you done to the breed? Now me, I'm just an ordinary man, besides being a murderer and a thief. Bad or good, like it or not, that's a natural thing for a man to be. But you see things different from the rest of us. I wouldn't trust you to go for a bucket of beer. You stay."

"Then what about my brother?"

Lowry looked at William Manning. "Brother's got a bad knee, case you forgot. Supposing the leg gets worse. Trinidad's a long way off. Ain't you never heard of gangrene? Your brother dies on the way to Trinidad, there would be a whole lot of delay. I made up my mind. I'm going to send the woman."

Alison Manning looked up and for the first time there was a spark of interest in her eyes. Up till now she had been staring into space.

"That's right, lady," Lowry said. "I'm going to send you."

Manning spoke quickly. "You'd be making a mistake if you did that."

"How so? She's your missus."

"And she hates my guts."

"What difference does that make? My boys will be with her."

Manning said, "Suppose she kicks up a row in front of the whole town? They've got a tough marshal there and he's got the backing of the townspeople. You've heard what he did to the McCargo brothers?"

"That I did, the sneaking bastard. You think this brings us back to sending you?"

"No," Manning said. "Sundance can go."

Lowry raised his eyebrows. "The breed! You must be soft in the head. You want to send a man you did your best to kill? Not just kill. You hunted him like an animal. Friend, you ever done that to me and I got away I'd find you somehow. Then I'd take you to a far place where they couldn't hear you scream. I'd have it all figured out what I was going to do to you so's I wouldn't get carried away and kill you by chance. I'd kill you for a month."

"That's why Sundance won't try to run out," Manning said. "You'd kill me if he got away."

"I might if I got mad enough." Lowry spat to show his contempt for Manning. "I knew I was right about you. You ain't said a thing about me killing your wife and brother."

"Slip of the tongue."

"Don't get too foxy. The slips are how you tell what a man's like. No matter. What you are is no business of mine. You say the breed can be trusted because he hates you so much. You say he'll get the money because he wants you turned loose so he can kill you his own way. I'll have to think about it. Guess it's about time I got that arrow out. Don't it hurt?"

"Not much," Manning answered. "I've had worse wounds."

"Well, so have I," Lowry said, going back to the jug. "But when I get wounded I squawk like a bastard. Now I'll just burn the blade of my knife so it's clean."

"Let Sundance do it," Manning said.

"You'd trust him with my knife at your chest?"

"He doesn't want to kill me that way."

"That right, breed?" Lowry asked. "All right. You take out the arrow, but you'll do it with my pistol in your ear. Make a wrong move and I'll splatter your brains all over this canyon. When you get done all you people can eat."

There was squirrel stew flavored with wild onions and seasoned with old rock salt. Lowry had gone into the ruined house to sleep off the whiskey. They were herded to a cockfire in the open and watched by Rufus and three other men while they ate. The jug had been passed around after Lowry went off to sleep, and now Rufus and the other guards were talking about what they planned to do with their share of the ransom money. The talk got louder all the time.

Sundance had taken the arrow from Manning's chest and bandaged the wound after washing it out with moonshine. The stew had a rank taste that not even the bitter onions could disguise, but they ate it greedily, wanting more but knowing they weren't going to get it. Alison Manning's face was streaked with dirt she hadn't bothered to wash off, though there was water going to waste in the spring. Sundance had seen it before. Ladies of breeding went to pieces faster than women who were accustomed to a tougher kind of life. There was bitterness in her eyes. She had retreated into silence.

Manning had been looking at Sundance. "We have to make a truce, the two of us," he said at last. "No matter how you feel, we have to talk about this. Later—if we survive—we can have it out."

"We'll have it out," Sundance said.

"It was none of my doing," William Manning said.

"It was—"

Sundance ignored him. So did his brother.

"A truce between us is the only hope," Manning went on. "They'll kill us as soon as they get the money. I think the old man will agree to let you go for it. He was leaning that way toward the end. Didn't you think so?"

Sundance hated to talk to Manning, but there was no way out of it. "Maybe," he said. "You want me to save your neck, is that it?"

"I think I made it possible for you to save your own neck. You have a chance of doing that if the old man sends you to Trinidad. You'll be guarded but he can't send too many men. I know you well by now. You'll find a way to get free."

"Most likely," Sundance said. "Then I'll be free and you'll be here. Then there's nothing to stop me from sending my own telegraph message to New York. To your banker. Saying you're dead and any other message he gets is a fraud. You'll be dead for sure when the old man knows he's out in the cold."

"We'll be dead too, Sundance," William Manning said.

"So you will." At the moment Sundance didn't much care what happened to William Manning or the woman. He knew they hadn't meant to kill him, yet they were too weak or confused to do anything about it.

"Why should I care what happens to you?" he said. "I have better things to do with my time. You wanted to play with danger. Now you have the chance, but you want to change your mind. The old man said it right. You're not so brave, Manning."

Manning said, "Never mind about me. What about my wife? She knew nothing about my plan. You'd let her die just to get back at me?"

"Don't try to hide behind me," Alison Manning said in a dead voice. "We're going to die in this rubbish pit. What's the use of taking about it? These savages have made up their minds."

"What's it going to be?" Manning asked Sundance. "If you get free, you can come back. They won't be expecting you. You're our only chance, and you know it."

"I'll kill you if I save your life," Sundance said. "That's the only reason I'll come back. What did you do to my horse?"

"I kept my word. I turned the stallion loose and headed him back toward that creek where we camped that night. There was grass there. The animal could survive."

"So you say."

"You would have heard a shot if I'd killed the stallion. William will tell you I'm speaking the truth. So will my wife."

Sundance looked at them and Alison Manning nodded. "He didn't kill your horse. You don't have to believe me. I don't care what you believe."

Sundance was more convinced by her apathy than he would have been by fervent avowals. What William Manning said didn't matter. Sundance felt a quickening of his heart at the thought that Eagle might be alive. For a long time he had accepted the fact that his great horse was dead, if not shot then dispatched by Baptiste's knife. One long thrust under the jawbone would do it.

"My horse better be alive," he warned Manning. "What I decide may depend on that. I don't know what I'm going to do. I'm like the old man. I have to think about it."

Rufus left off joking with the other guards and came

to the campfire. He couldn't hold as much whiskey as his father. He was drunk and grinning. The other guards watched him and Sundance knew that what they did depended on what Rufus did.

"The lady's et her fill and ought to take a nap," Rufus said.

Sundance stood up. "The lady's not tired."

Rufus pulled his gun and cocked it. He wasn't half as fast as his father. But it didn't matter how fast he was; he had the gun.

"I could bend this across your red-nigger nose," Rufus said. "Now you squat down in the dirt like you was doing whilst I take the little lady for her nap. What're you fussing about anyhow? She's had a stiff one in her afore today."

"No," Sundance said.

"You keep saying that," Rufus said. "You don't know how to say something else?"

"Your old man won't like this."

"My old man ain't here."

Rufus was still grinning when a bullet took away the top of his ear. It spurted blood as all ear wounds do, more so than any other kind. Rufus whirled with the cocked pistol in his hand. The blood still spattered on his shirt.

"Try it, you dumb son of a bitch," his father said from the porch. "A long time I been looking for a reason to kill you. This and that wasn't enough. You'd like to head up this gang. Here's your chance."

Rufus's eyes were wild with pain and anger. "You keep riding me, Lowry. All the time you don't do nothing else."

"Holster that pistol or use it." The gun in the old man's hand was rock steady. "No more talk, sonny boy. I'm so sick of you I could puke. All right, son of mine. I'll come down and make up your mind for you.''

"Stay off," Rufus yelled. "You ain't going to slap me in front of these people. You done that too many times and you ain't going to do it no more."

Lowry stepped down from the porch and kept coming, walking straight into the cocked pistol held by his son. He strode past the guards, ignoring them as if they hadn't been there. It could go any way, Sundance knew. They all wanted the woman. Rufus hesitated an instant too long, and then he didn't have a chance. The old man's pistol jabbed hard into his belly and he jack-knifed. Then the pistol hit him again, this time across the top of the head. Lowry spun around before his son hit the ground.

"What's the matter, boys? Lose your nerve? There's still three of you and one of me."

One of them spoke. "Wasn't us that started up with the woman, Lowry. You said hands off so we kept 'em off. How was we to know Rufus'd get horny so fast?"

Lowry spat on the man's boots. "What you know is what I tell you, Deakins. Same thing goes for the rest of you mongrels. Goddamn it to hell! Where are the men I used to ride with in the old days? Was a time I'd be shamed to be seen with the likes of you. Now you take this pig son of mine and get him out of my sight. Don't do nothing to bring him to, hear me. I hope he dies."

Rufus groaned and rolled over on his back. The old man spat tobacco juice in his face. "Just my luck the son of a bitch ain't dead. Take him away from here, Deakins. You stay away too. All of you stay away."

Deakins looked at Rufus rolling on the ground and trying to get the tobacco spit out of his eyes. "Why are you so mad, Lowry? Rufus is your kin, these people ain't a thing to you."

Lowry snapped his store teeth together. "These people here is the closest kin I know. These new kin of mine, like my marriage, is going to bring me health and happiness and the kind of old age every man dreams of. That's money, Deakins. You ain't going to have no old age, but I'll tell you anyhow. It's a secret of how to get things done. When you have people just where you want them, don't push them harder than you have to. Raping the lady might have done just that."

Deakins and the other guards lifted Rufus to his feet and carried him away. It was quiet in the canyon because no wind reached there. The spring bubbled out of the rock, so the only sound was the spring and the horses moving in the corral. They waited for Lowry to say something. Finally he did.

"The breed goes for the money."

CHAPTER SEVEN

"But he's got to look spiffy," Lowry said, holding his head with both hands. "Right now he looks as if the wrath of God has been visited upon him. No banker—I don't care what you say—would give the breed a red cent, the way he looks. I'd give him a dime or even a dollar because I'm a man of Christian charity. More or less I am. Anyway, I'm a man of kindly inclination, and never you mind the bad company I keep."

They were on the porch again and Lowry was passing the jug. "You must be a reformed sinner," he said to William Manning, who had refused a drink. "On t'other hand it ain't hard to see how a man would want to swear off warm moonshine even when it's cut and cooled by spring water. You good people get enough to eat, did you?"

"It was all right," Manning said.

Lowry hiccupped and blew out whiskey fumes. "No it wasn't. We'll have a real feed when the breed gets back from Trinidad with the money. My money. I ask you this. What's to stop the breed from bringing back every kind of good thing to eat? My boys and the breed. Course there's no way to bring fresh cow meat that distance, but what I'm thinking about is grub in cans. Corned beef in cans. Tomatoes in cans. Peaches in all kind of sugary shit. All that don't mean much to you people, but I got a craving for civilized food. You won't let me down, will you, half breed?"

"Just tell me what you want," Sundance said.

"We got to get some decent looking clothes for you," Lowry said. "What you got on a scarecrow would say no to. You sure you know how to read and write?"

"Pretty good," Sundance said.

"Well, I'll be damned to the eternal fires of hell," Lowry said. "A halfbreed that can read and write. Just remember this. The boys that go along with you can do the same. They know how to do it, so don't go trying to do nothing else than what you're supposed to. Understand me?"

Sundance nodded. "What you say is what gets done."

"I kind of like you," Lowry said. "You may be a breed, but you're more my people than these people. These foreigners."

Sundance said thanks.

"Well, it's true," Lowry said. "Course you ain't American like me. What the hell, I like you anyhow."

Sundance said, "How soon do I go?"

"In a hurry, are you?"

"The sooner gone, the sooner back."

The old man whipped out his pistol. "You talk as foxy as the Englishman. Try to. Say you're just a red nigger that picks up tricks like a tame crow. Say it."

"Go bull yourself, Lowry."

The old bandit grinned. "How's that again, half-breed?"

"You heard."

Lowry holstered his gun and grinned. "So I did. Nerve is something I admire in a man, be he nigger or a

92

red nigger or white like me. Men these days is losing their nerve all over the place. I got some good clothes for you, Sundance. They seen you in Trinidad, is that right?"

"That marshal saw me. A lot of other people."

"Then you leave come morning. You know what's for supper?"

"Squirrel stew?"

"Fried squirrel," Lowry said. "Same difference. All tastes as bad. But there's good times coming. You and me, Sundance. How come you don't want a drink, bad as it is?"

"Bad for me, Lowry."

"Bad for you, then bad for me. As a usual thing it's bad for me too. Why is that? I get wild when I drink too much. Why is that, my red brother?"

Lowry lurched away before he heard Sundance's answer. He didn't close the door to the house because there was no door.

"You've made a hit with him, Sundance," Manning said. "I tried but I couldn't. You did. That's good."

"He's better than you are, Manning. Anybody is better than you."

"A harsh judgment but probably true. You didn't suck up to him."

"You did."

"Is that what I was doing?"

"Sounded like it."

"You have a lot to learn," Manning said.

Some of Manning's talkiness had returned now that he knew he had a chance to live.

Sure, Sundance thought, the bastard thinks I'll be bigger game if I can bring this off. That was all right because Manning had failed—even failed in the old bandit's eyes—and no matter what he did after this—knowing his failure—he wouldn't be the same. Cracks had appeared in the steely front he showed to the world. No matter what he did to repair them, the cracks would remain. The flaws that had betrayed him.

"I know all about you that I have to know," Sundance said.

"You saw what my son is like," Lowry said after he ordered them into the ruined house. "So I hope there ain't going to be any delays with the money. My money. If the money is too long coming, I may not be able to hold my boys in line. Fact is, I ain't going to try too hard. The lady won't be a lady when the boys get through with her. I'm talking to you, the husband."

"You'll get the money," Manning said.

"Sure I will, but there's a few precautions we got to take. First thing is, the breed can't go looking like he is. Guess we can fix him up with some half decent clothes, then feed him up for a day or two so's he won't look like he'd been hung and cut down just in time. Second thing, what happens if this New York banker decides to ask questions about how you need so much cash money?"

"He's not supposed to ask questions," Manning said. "That was the arrangement. He knows the kind of life I lead, the wild places I go."

Lowry grinned, crafty as ever. "But suppose he ain't there when the telegraph comes? Could be sick in bed with the grippe."

"That's all been taken care of," Manning said. "The money will be sent or he'll find himself looking for another job. I have a lot of investments in this country, so he'll know better than to keep me waiting. Why should I tell you lies when you have a gun to my head?''

Lowry rinsed his mouth with spring water before he swallowed it. ''Nothing like warm moonshine to bust a man's skull. This banker know about the breed?''

Manning nodded. ''He knows I hired Sundance. We talked about it. The bank manager knows Sundance's reputation for fair play.''

''Too bad he didn't know about yours,'' Lowry said. ''Course I ain't got no complaints on that score. I'll be a rich man the first time in my life. You don't know what it's like to be pore. Well, like I told you, it makes a man wild with the hunger for money.''

''I understand,'' Manning said.

''Do you now? Right now I'm finished talking with you, Englishman. All of you clear out 'cepting the breed. I got a few things to say to him. There's part of a jug left on the porch. Drink it up if you like. Now waltz on out of here. Go sit by the fire.''

''I don't like that feller,'' Lowry said after the Mannings went out. ''You get enough to eat out there?''

''For now,'' Sundance answered. He didn't ask Lowry what he wanted to talk about; there was no way to hurry the old bandit.

''I got to root out some clothes for you,'' Lowry said, rinsing his mouth again. ''You think I don't know what you're up to?''

A chipmunk twittered in the part of the roof that had collapsed. A shower of dust came down and hung for a while in the bright sunlight.

''What am I up to?''

''A doublecross. That's what you're up to. You'd be a goddamned fool if you didn't think about it. What I mean is, here's this crazy rich man that tried to kill you, and here you are with the power of life and death over him. Let me finish what I'm saying. You figure to get the drop on my boys soon as the money comes in. If you can do that, you're a rich man and the foreigner is a dead man. They're all dead and you're gone with the money.''

"It's a thought.''

"A foolish thought. The boys that go with you will be my best. They'll blow you apart in the telegraph office if they have to. You'll have a carbine and a belt gun, but they'll be empty.''

Sundance said, "Then why would I try something?''

"'Cause I can't see any man not wanting to steal a hundred thousand dollars. But you'll get the money and my boys will take it from you. They'll bring it back here because they know I'd find them if they didn't. But just suppose you did make off with the money. If you did that, you'd find yourself hunted for kidnaping and murder. Wouldn't be no trouble to get the story passed around. You murdered them in the mountains, is how the story would go.''

"You have something better in mind?''

"A lot better for you. Get the money, make no trouble, and you go free the minute my boys have it in their hands. You go free right there in Trinidad. And so's you don't walk away empty-handed, you'll get ten thousand dollars. Nothing's going to happen to you once my boys get the money. They'd be fools to kill you in town, what with all that money at stake. That's a good offer, mister.''

Sundance pretended to think about it, knowing that there was a good chance of staying alive if he passed over the ransom money. If they shot him in town they'd have a posse on their heels in five minutes.

"You're thinking about the Englishman, ain't you?''

Lowry said.

"He's got a few things coming to him," Sundance said. "I'd like to see he got them."

"He'll get them. That's my promise to you. Part of the deal, if you like. The others I'll just kill. The Englishman I'll kill slow. That won't be hard to do, seeing how he is. Course you can always come back here with the boys."

"No thanks," Sundance said. "There's only one thing you left out."

"What's that?"

"How do you know I won't go to the law after I get free?"

"Now why would you want to do that? I ain't done you no harm. I'm letting you go free with clothes on your back, money in your pocket. So why would you want to do me an injury? These foreigners can't mean a thing to you. Besides, the law wouldn't believe you. You're a breed in a white man's country. Take my word for it. The law likes a bird in the hand. You'd be the bird. Now we talked enough. That's my offer. Take it or leave it."

"I'll take it," Sundance said.

"See, you ain't so dumb," Lowry said. "Now go sit by the fire while I have a talk with the boys."

Alison Manning was the only one drinking moonshine at the fire. She looked up at Sundance with dull eyes before she tilted the jug again.

"You'll be sick as a dog if you drink much more of that," Sundance said.

"Who the hell cares?" she said. "I'm not sick now."

"What did he want?" Manning asked. "Are you still

97

going for the money?''

Sundance said, ''He offered to let me go if I didn't make trouble. It's worth it to him.''

Manning's voice remained calm. ''What did you say?''

''I said yes. I think he believed me.''

Night was coming on and the canyon was deeply shadowed. The spring flowed inexhaustibly from the rock.

Manning glanced at the ruined house. There was light in it now. ''How are you going to do it?'' he said.

''Do what?''

''Get us out of here?''

''I don't know how I'm going to do it. I won't be doing it for you.''

''Perhaps you are. You want to get me out so you can take your revenge.''

''Let that go, your wife is here,'' Sundance said.

''Don't mind me,'' Manning's wife said. ''But watch out for my dear husband. He may try to sell you to the old man. There's no telling what Edward will do.''

Sundance said, ''It wouldn't do him any good. The old man won't let him go no matter what happens.''

''Yes,'' Manning said. ''But how are you going to do it? When will you come back?''

''Before the old man gets mad enough to kill you. All you can do is be ready when I get here. If we can run off their horses maybe there's a chance. You won't be under too much of a guard because they know you can't get far. Be ready to move, that's all. Be ready to die.''

Lowry came out of the house with Rufus and three other men trailing behind him. They were arguing about something and the old man roared them into silence. Then he waved them away and came over to the fire, rubbing his hands against the evening chill.

"You people can sleep over there." He pointed. "Under the lee of the cliff. You'll be watched the night through so don't try to wander off. After this you do your own cooking. I just set Rufus and the boys straight. About the lady, is what I mean. You won't get no botheration there. Now come get your blankets."

Now that Manning was in danger, his wife was no longer afraid of him. In the shadow of death she was free for a little while, and she made up her bed as far away from him as she could get. The blankets were dirty but heavy enough; out of the wind it wasn't too cold. The light in the house went out and after that there was no sound except the flow of the spring. Lying in his blankets Sundance watched the glow of cigarettes as the guards smoked in the dark. He knew there was no telling how it would go. In the end there was no one he could trust. The Mannings, whatever they were, made up some kind of family. So did Lowry and his gang. He was the outsider here. If he looked at it sensibly he owed no loyalty to anyone. The smart thing would be to get away as best he could and leave them to what the old man would dish out to them. There was a lot more involved than the lives of three people who had never done anything of value since the day they were born. He thought of all the Indians—white people too—who lived on the edge of starvation, so it was hard to worry about the plight of the Mannings. It was hard to believe that saving their lives would make any change in their lives. He didn't think his own life was so valuable except where it concerned the Indians he was trying to help. What sense did it make if he got killed?

It was late when he heard someone crawling toward him in the darkness. His hand reached for the sharp rock that lay beside him, the only weapon he had.

"Sundance," Alison Manning whispered. "Are you awake?"

She was close enough so that he could cover her mouth with his hand. There was no struggle when he did it. One of the guards yawned long and loud.

"You could get shot," Sundance whispered. "What do you want?"

"I have to tell you something. You're going to get one hundred thousand that isn't there. My husband can't raise that much money. There's the house and the land in England, but that's all. Perhaps it's worth that much money, but he doesn't have it in New York. Are you listening to me? Edward has lost most of his money in wild ventures. If you go to Trinidad you'll be killed. There's no money."

"I hear you," Sundance said. "Why are you telling me this?"

"Because he's tried to trick you again. He agreed to the old man's demands because it meant a few more weeks of life. Not for me, not for his brother—for himself. Because he's counting on the kind of man you are."

Sundance knew she could be lying. He knew it could be Manning's idea, something that would put him in her debt, something that would make him want to save her. These people were so full of twists and turns that everything they said had to be regarded with suspicion.

"You're giving me a good reason to duck out on you," he said.

No more than fifteen feet away William Manning cried out in his sleep. It sounded like that. Sundance wasn't sure.

"Duck out if you like, if you can," Alison Manning

whispered. "What happens to us is of no consequence. Do what you like. I'm just telling you."

"Thanks for that. Go back now before somebody catches on you're here."

"What are you going to do?"

"Think about it. It doesn't change much. I never meant to go all the way to Trinidad."

She whispered, "How many men will go with you?"

"The old man didn't say. You mean how many men I will draw away from here?"

Angered by the question she was ready to curse him. He clapped his hand over her mouth just in time.

"I'm not in a trusting mood," he said. "I'll get you out of here if I can. Then you can go to hell."

He took his hand away from her mouth.

"Another hero," she hissed. "I'm so sick of all you bloody heroes."

Sundance smiled at her as she crawled away. She was right about heroes. The world had too many heroes and not enough sensible cowards.

CHAPTER EIGHT

In the morning Sundance watched for some sign that the old man knew something about his visit from Alison Manning. But there was none, so he guessed Lowry didn't know about it. In all his life he had never been caught in such a web of suspicion and mistrust. Cookfires were going before he rolled out of his blankets. He had been awake for a long time, but there was nothing to get up for.

Lowry was down by the creek soaking his whiskey head in cold water when he went there to drink, then later to wash himself downstream. Birds singing in the canyon gave the place a pleasant sound. The Mannings hadn't turned out yet.

"Morning," Lowry said. "Lordy me, but don't I have a skullbuster this fine day. Soon as I get my money and get far from here, I'm going to drink nothing but the best. You think that'll help?"

The water was good and Sundance drank a lot of it. "Not much," he said. "Liquor is liquor. Drink enough and you get a head."

"I been told that one time by a doctor when I had the shakes. Still and all, a man can take pride in being laid low by good liquor. Used to be a drinker and give it up, did you? Where you from anyways? I'm from southern

103

Missouri, but ain't been back there a lot of years. I'd like to go back and die there when my time comes, only I ain't 'cause you might follow me there and do me in."

"No special reason to do that."

"Good for you. Whereabouts you going with your money?"

"All over."

"Best place to go. They can't catch up with you there. You'll be leaving for Trinidad today."

"I thought a few days."

"Today. I keep changing things. That's my way. You'd do the same, am I wrong?"

"No. Not in your business," Sundance said. "It'll take a full week to get there. We took longer to get up this way, but we dallied—the hunting."

"Oh yes, that," Lowry said. "You look all right to leave today. I don't mind you, Sundance, not a bit. You're ever down to Missouri, come and visit now."

Sundance grinned at the bandit. "Tell me where," he said.

Lowry grinned back. "None of your business, but if you can find me, the latchstring will be out."

"Or your gun?"

"Don't be like that, my friend. There's prosperous times coming to us all. Not to mention your fancy foreigner friends."

"No friends of mine."

"Don't tell me you don't like her? Like hell and damnation you don't. I'd like to keep her as a pet, cover them freckles with rice powder and show her off to the folks wherever I'm taking my money. Not Missouri. I like pale women. They're the ones got the spirit, not them leather-faced farm women in poke bonnets and talk rough and can't cook nothing but greasy."

Sundance saw Alison Manning coming down from the shelter of the cliff. "Here's your chance," he said.

"Nice woman like that got a dirty face. Can't you tell her to wash it? All the time I see her I'm thinking such a shame to kill her. You don't think the same?"

"Not so much I want to die here with her. Let her wash her face or not—"

"Call me Lowry," the old man said.

"Morning, ma'am," he said to Alison Manning. "The accommodations wasn't too bad, I hope?"

She muttered something. After the old man went back to the house, she went to the pool below the spring and washed her face and neck. Sundance watched her while she combed her hair, working twigs and grass out of it.

"I'm going today," Sundance said. "The old man just told me. I guess you were on the level last night. You took a chance to tell me."

There were a few streaks of gray in her hair that he hadn't noticed before, though she couldn't have been more than thirty. "You believe me then?" she asked.

He nodded. "I did after I thought about it. Stick close to the old man while I'm away. The one called Rufus will be coming with me, so there won't be any trouble with him. I don't know how many others will be guarding me. I guess three."

She began to coil her hair and fix it with pins. "You'll have to kill them, won't you?"

"If I can."

Manning's wife shuddered in the morning shadows. The sun wasn't warm yet. "It would be pleasant here if not for—" She made a sort of hopeless gesture. "I'm sorry you have to be a part of this."

"So am I," Sundance said, turning to see what the

old man wanted. He was yelling from the porch.

"Time to get fancied up," the old man called. "The lady can cook your breakfast while you're getting dressed."

There was a fairly clean shirt, a pair of canvas pants, and a hat with two holes in it. "There's your pistol and belt," Lowry said. "The boys are getting a horse. But no knife, like I said. You're too handy with a knife. You got everything clear in your head, or do I have to say it again?"

Sundance said no. "The woman will be all right?"

"All right in the way you mean. Don't fret about her. She won't feel a thing when her time comes. You have my word on that. You want to know who's going with you? Well sir, there's my hateful son Rufus. Then there's Deakins, Leggett, and Johnson. They'll be along directly. Don't mess with those boys, Sundance. They got their orders. Get fed and get going."

Alison Manning was frying squirrel meat when Sundance went back to the cliff. There was too much fire under the skillet and he took it away from her and raked a bed of coals. "You'll never make a cook," he said.

"I wouldn't mind being a cook," she said. "I wouldn't mind being anything except what I am. You look terrible in those clothes."

"Don't I know it." Sundance looked at Edward Manning. "If I get back I'll come down the canyon wall in the dark. Don't sleep too sound. One more thing. Don't try to escape. You're no match for these men. Wait for me and maybe we'll get out. No matter what I tell you to do, you'll do it. I know how you think the world should be run, but this is my world here, not yours."

Manning crunched a piece of burned squirrel meat between his strong, white teeth. "Well, you're the guide, aren't you?"

Four men on horses rode up from the corral. Rufus was leading the horse for Sundance. Lowry came down from the house. Dust churned up by the horses was heavy in the air and the sun was edging over the rim of the canyon.

Lowry pointed at his mean-faced son. "Get back in two weeks, boy. Stay later than that and I'll come looking for you. All you fellers remember that. Run to Old Mexico, go clear to South America, and I'll still find you. You'll never have a minute's peace if you run out on me."

"Sure, Lowry," Rufus said. "Two weeks you said and that's what you'll get."

"Be off," the old man roared.

Sundance mounted up and they rode out of the canyon past the guards at the far end. He was riding east again, back over all the miles he had been hunted. There was the long-barreled .44 Colt riding on his hip, but he was pretty sure the old man had removed the firing pin. It was the sort of thing the old man would do.

Out of the canyon it was hot. The sun was beating down on the rocks and brush. There was plenty of water for the long journey ahead. Rufus and Deakins rode behind him, the others in front. The horses' flanks were shiny as they rode. Sundance's horse was a sturdy Morgan but not so young that it could make any distance if he tried to make a run for it. He saw the old man's hand in that too. The sun was a pitiless blue with a few wisps of cloud drifting up very high. The desert and the mountains they would have to cross lay ahead.

In an hour they came to the place where he had tried

to kill Manning. Baptiste's body lay in the dust with buzzards flapping around it. They hadn't finished yet but they were well on their way. They had clawed and torn the shirt away and were working on the belly. Baptiste's face was gone and there was a bad smell. Rufus spat and killed two buzzards with two shots.

Deakins said, "What the hell's the matter with you, Rufe? Lowry said do nothing to get noticed."

"Old man ain't here," Rufus said. "Anyhow, who's going to hear shooting out here?"

"It's just dumb doing that," Deakins complained.

Rufus, slack-jawed, stared at him while he pushed two shells into his revolver. "Let's not be giving orders. I'm in charge here and you ain't. 'Lessen the old man told you something different, I'm in charge. You got something else you want to say?"

"Nothing, Rufe," Deakins said.

"That's the right thing to say," Rufus said. "Let's go get the money. I can't hardly wait to be rich."

This time there would be no way to fashion homemade weapons, Sundance knew. What he killed with would have to be seized or stolen. He guessed there wouldn't be any stealing, so it would have to be sudden. There was friction between Rufus and Deakins, and that was something to think about. The other two men, Leggett and Johnson, didn't talk at all, so it looked like the old man had picked men who weren't likely to team up.

Making good time, they reached the desert by noon, the hottest part of the day. Rufus's tuneless whistle broke off when he saw what lay ahead of them.

"It's going to be a bitch out there," he complained. "What I'd like now is a cold bottle of beer."

"Me too," Deakins agreed. "You mind me asking

how the split is going to go? Was no mention of that by your father."

"What you get is more than you have," Rufus said. "If you think Lowry talked it over with me, you're wrong. He don't talk over nothing with me. It was me seen them flares in the sky while Lowry was sleeping off his moon. You'd think that'd count for something."

"I seen them too," Deakins said. "The other guards thought they meant some kind of army patrol. I knew they wasn't."

Rufus looked sideways at him. "How could you know that? Miles from where they was, how could you tell?"

"Easy. If the army was after us, it would be like giving us a signal. The other guards got jumpy. I wasn't one bit jumpy."

"We was all jumpy," Rufus said. "Which means that you was too. The only one that wasn't jumpy was Lowry. That old man never gets jumpy."

"He says plenty of hard things to you," Deakins said.

"What's that got to do with it?"

"Well, you're his own flesh and blood and he talks meaner to you than the rest of us. Now if I had a son—"

"You ain't got no son, Deakins."

"Not that I know of, Rufe."

Rufus winked at Deakins. "You got any brats, Sundance?"

Sundance said no.

Rufus said, "Just as well. They wouldn't be too smart, seeing as how you ain't so smart. How'd you ever let yourself get took in by that Englishman? Lowry says how could you tell he was going to do what he did. I think different. I think you was dumb."

Deakins said, "Funny thing, Rufe. Lowry likes the

breed and he don't like nobody. Lowry says the breed is going to play it straight."

"What else can he do, a dumb breed like he is? You are going to play it straight, ain't you?"

"We made a deal," Sundance said.

Rufus gave a sniggering laugh that was just like the rest of him. "You ain't made a deal with us."

Sundance knew they were taking out their fear on him. As bandits they were small potatoes, men who stole and killed and ran to a safe place. To them a village bank with a few thousand in the cash drawer was like the Denver Mint. Chance had promoted them to the hundred thousand dollar class and they didn't know how to handle it. What they were doing now was something they hadn't done before, not even in their whiskey dreams, and it confused them. The old man, bad as he was, was better than they were, and Sundance was glad he wasn't along for the ride. Killing the old man would not have been easy.

Now they were crossing the ancient lava beds that sloped down into the desert. After a year of bad food and moonshine they were in no condition to take it. Sweat soaked Rufus's shirt and dribbled from his chin.

"Look at the breed," he said to Deakins. "That breed don't hardly even sweat."

Deakins sleeved sweat from his face. "Breeds ain't human, that's why. They can live on things would make a white man puke to look at. Now the full-blooded Injun ain't such a bad feller. He's a dumb animal, but there's ways about him you can sort of respect. A breed ain't nothing like that. It's the breeds I hate more than anything."

"Me too," Rufus said.

In the early afternoon they rested in the shade of a

giant cactus and ate dried meat and drank water. The desert was hot and white in the sun. Rufus drew his pistol to kill a harmless ring-necked snake, but changed his mind and set down the hammer. Far away they could see the mountains, jagged and brown.

"I'll wager Lowry's dipping into the moon pretty good by now," Deakins said. "Sitting on the porch in the shade, a jug and good cold water at his elbow. Soon as he gets enough in his belly he'll sleep the afternoon away, then start again till it's time for bed."

"That's because he's the boss," Rufus said. "But you're right. I wouldn't mind being back there now, jawing with Lowry and him jawing back at me."

"Was surprised Lowry didn't let you have a go at that woman. I know your daddy is on the old side for the ladies. That didn't mean you couldn't have given her a little bit. A little for you, a little for him."

Rufus laughed. "And a little for you."

"I'd get my little for myself," Deakins said.

Nothing was said that Sundance hadn't heard before: the same old talk of stupid, cowardly bullies. Men who hated their betters. Anyone was better than they were. Rufus was worse than Deakins, but Deakins was smarter in his shifty, country-talking way. Any backwoods dance turned up a lot of men like Deakins. A saloon on Saturday night was full of them. Five foot eight and wanting to be taller and resenting it because he wasn't, in a land where all tall men were said to be brave, Deakins was a man lacking resolution or any kind of real courage. He was a dark little man with quick eyes always seeking opportunity, sometimes finding it and always losing it, because he didn't know it when he saw it, or throwing it away because he was forever dissatisfied, and didn't think it was good enough for him.

A sneaky little shit kicker, Sundance thought. The world was too crowded with men like that. He thought he could work on Deakins, a dangerous man with a mind like a corkscrew. Deakins was clever enough to know that he wasn't going to get a fair share from old Lowry. He might even have figured that Lowry planned to doublecross everybody, even his own son, or especially his own son. To Sundance that had come through all the rambling about going back to Missouri. Of course he wouldn't go to Missouri. Mexico or Central America was where the old man intended to run. There he could put himself under the protection of some powerful politician and live the life of a gentleman. Once he had bought Mexican citizenship, there was no one who could touch him, not even the Pinkertons.

Sundance knew he had to get back long before the two-week time limit laid down by the old man. If he cut it too close the old man would be watching for them night and day. They'd all be watching, stirring in their sleep, thinking of the money. If he delayed too long they might go after the woman and Lowry would try to stop them, not because there was any goodness in him, but because once he lost control he would never get it back. If the others killed the old man they might kill the Mannings just to get it done. Naturally the woman would be the last to die.

"Best to be moving on," Rufus said. "I'm still thinking of that cold beer."

The desert was behind them by the end of the following day, and the air grew cooler as they climbed out of it. They made camp in the foothills.

"Let the breed make the fire," Rufus said. "He ain't going to run. We'll put a hobble on him. Snake out a rope and tie it about his ankles. Keep a tight hold on the other end."

Sundance stood up with the rope biting into his flesh. It will be good to kill them, he thought.

"Get a move on," Rufus said, then grabbed the rope and brought Sundance crashing down.

"That's dumb work," Deakins said. "He could have split his head on a rock. Fun's fun, but we got to think of the money. You cripple the breed and there ain't going to be no money. You want to go back and explain to Lowry how that happened?"

"Start the goddamned fire. I'm hungry. And don't go bringing up Lowry all the time. You're going to get me mad if you keep it up."

Later, Rufus sat warming his hands at the fire. There was a pale moon and it was cold. Leggett and Johnson drank their coffee and said nothing. The hobbled horses browsed on dry yellow grass. Far below, coyotes howled in the desert.

"Well, this ain't so bad," Rufus said. "I feel so good I'm going to have me a drink. Don't tell me what Lowry said, Deakins. I snuck off a bottle or two while Lowry wasn't looking."

Deakins looked at Sundance. "I don't want a drink," he said.

Rufus got a bottle of moonshine from his saddlebag. "Nobody asked you, preacher. All you got to do is make sure the breed is roped good and tight. Used to be a cow nurse, didn't you?"

"I worked at that. Other things too."

"Then you know about ropes. Rope him now. I like to be safe when I drink."

Deakins roped Sundance's ankles together, then turned him on his side and bent his legs behind him.

After that he tied his wrists and attached the end of the rope to his ankles.

"He won't run now," Deakins said, testing the ropes before he poured water on the knots to keep them hard.

"That's the idea," Rufus said. "You don't want a drink so you ain't going to get none. How about you two fellers? Man hates to drink alone. That's how a man gets to be a drunkard, I'm told."

Leggett and Johnson said they'd have a drink. "Then hold out your cups," Rufus said. "You get a full cup apiece and the rest is for me. Course I might give you another cup when I get to feeling generous. A good thing friend Deakins don't feel like drinking. That leaves more for the rest of us. Friend Deakins won't want to drink 'cause he's worried about the money. Course it ain't his money, but that don't stop him from worrying."

Leggett and Johnson gulped the raw moonshine and sat in moody silence. The fire crackled, sending up sparks. Rufus tilted the bottle again and again. Sundance lay on his side, feeling the heat of the fire on his back.

"I keep on thinking about that Englishwoman," Rufus said, slurring his words. "That lady ain't got big tits. What she has is nice and solid. A man could throw his lips over either one of them and suck to his heart's content. A man could ride her all night and still want more in the morning. Am I right, boys?"

"Sure," Johnson said. "I mean you're right."

"Ain't you got nothing to say, Leggett? Sure is hard to carry on a conversation with you men. Leggett, my friend, it don't cost nothing to talk. You ain't being charged by the word."

"Sure," Leggett said, eyeing the bottle. "You feeling

generous yet, Rufus?"

"Not yet," Rufus said. "What I am feeling is kind of sleepy. Tell you what though. I'll sell you a drink at five dollars a cup. I know you ain't got no money right now. You will when you get your share. You got good credit with me, boys."

"I'll take a cup," Johnson said.

In a while they were all asleep except Sundance and Deakins.

"You mind turning me the other way?" Sundance said quietly. "You tied me hard and I'm getting cramped up."

Deakins tested the ropes before he turned Sundance toward the fire.

Sundance said, "I heard you talking to Rufus about your share of the money. You think you're going to get it?"

Deakins kicked at a blazing brand that had fallen close to his foot. His small dark eyes flickered uneasily. "That's got nothing to do with you."

"Maybe it has. I have the old man's word I'll get ten thousand and go free. He'll keep his word because he wants the law looking for me instead of him."

"Then you have his word."

"Rufus will break it for him. That's because Rufus is dumb and greedy. Who's to know what's happened to me after I'm buried deep and Rufus has my ten thousand?"

Deakins said, "Who's to know? Who's to care?" He glanced over at Rufus, who was groaning in his sleep. "Rufe can't take your ten thousand and kill you without the rest of us knowing about it. To keep us from telling the old man he'll have to give us equal shares. Twenty-five hundred ain't so bad on top of the other we get. You're dead and we're rich and the old man thinks you're in Texas or Montana."

"How about the Pinkertons? Where will they think I am? If they don't find me, they'll start looking for you."

Deakins stared into the fire. "Looking for Lowry, you mean?"

"Looking for all of you."

"Not me. Soon as I get my share I'm going to cut loose from Lowry. I'm not a well-known man. They won't be looking too hard for me."

"Then you don't know the Pinkertons. You think you can murder these three people and get away with it? You think people that can raise a hundred thousand won't have family and important friends out looking to catch their killers?"

"I ain't going to take part in it," Deakins said.

"They'll hang you just the same," Sundance said. "It won't make any difference to the law who does the murders."

"Then what difference does it make? The only reason I'm listening, I want to hear what's in your sneaky brain. You're forgetting they'll have to catch me before they hang me."

Sundance said, "They'll catch you faster than Lowry. Money talks on both sides of the law. And Lowry will have plenty of that. How much will you have? A few thousand, if you don't get cheated out of that. Not enough to get very far. When the word goes out on you, you won't find many places to hide. Everything will suddenly cost you ten times as much. Then there's the reward money. It'll be dead or alive, you know that. Mostly it'll be dead. Bounty hunters like to keep it simple."

Deakins's thin mouth twitched with anger. "You got a lot to say, for a breed. I can shut you up any time."

"What does it cost you to listen? There's only one way you can get clear of this, and that's money. You don't even know that Rufus doesn't plan to pull a doublecross on the way back to the canyon."

"Keep your damn voice down," Deakins snarled. His own voice was louder than Sundance's. "What are you trying to say?"

"That we pull our own doublecross before Rufus pulls his. Two of us, three of them. You down Leggett and Johnson, I'll kill Rufus. Then we go collect the money."

Deakins gave out with an evil grin. "Then you down me and make off with everything?"

"Or you kill me and you're set for life. Or we play it square and divvy up the hundred thousand. Fifty thousand would take you beyond the reach of Lowry or the law. You have a better chance with me than anybody. I'm no killer."

"Just a thief."

"A thief that was forced into it. I started out to guide some people and ended up running for my life. No food, no weapons, a crazy man with a scoped rifle at my back. You think I don't have a right to something?"

"Not everything. Lowry said you're fast with a gun. Lowry said we'd have to watch you every minute. I put a gun in your hand I could be dead. I don't doubt you're fast. I can tell."

"You could kill them right now," Sundance said. "Three bullets and it's over. No need to give me a gun after that. Just walk me into Trinidad with an empty gun in my holster. All it takes is nerve."

Deakins didn't like having his nerve questioned. He

licked his lips and looked at the sleeping men. "I could kill them and then kill you last," he said. "You'd be easy to kill, all trussed up like you are. You think I couldn't send for the money myself? You got the information written down."

"The people in Trinidad have seen me with the Englishman. They know I work for him. They know I'm no outlaw. What will they say when they see you by yourself? Kill them now and take me under guard. It's a better chance than what you have now."

Sundance knew there was real danger in putting thoughts of murder into Deakins's head. Like all penny ante thieves Deakins dreamed that some fine morning he would wake up and find himself rich. Then he could swagger for the women who had never noticed him before. He looked like the kind of gutless little rat that yearned for the respect of men with respect. His lack of courage made him dangerous, and his greed made him more so.

"How about it?" Sundance asked. "You may not get a better chance."

Deakins drew his gun and he was pretty fast. But he didn't thumb back the hammer. It was all for show. "Shut your stinking mouth," he hissed. "If I told Rufus—"

"But you won't." Sundance wasn't sure he wouldn't. Anything could happen with this bunch of men.

"Say another word and I'll gag you," Deakins said.

Leggett and Johnson guarded Sundance, in two watches, for the rest of the night. Sundance slept and Rufus was still snoring when he woke before dawn. Johnson was on the last watch and he made the fire and put the coffee on to boil.

Cursing and groaning, Rufus woke up with a sick

head. He rinsed his mouth with coffee and spat. Then he poured moonshine into his coffee and drank it quickly, holding the breath to keep from throwing up.

"What're you gawking at?" he said to Deakins. "Can't a man have a few drinks without you looking at him like a dead fish?"

"I didn't say a word, Rufe," Deakins answered.

Rufus helped himself to more coffee, this time without the moon. "You didn't have to," he said. "How come you untied the breed without me telling you?"

"He can't eat with his hands roped behind his back."

"The hell with how he eats. How come you didn't call me for my watch?"

"You were sleeping sound, Rufe. I stood your watch for you. Wasn't no big favor."

"Who said it was?" Rufus said, spitting again. "Maybe you're trying to say I was too drunk? Maybe that's what you'll try to tell Lowry when we get back?"

"I wasn't sleepy, is all," Deakins said. "Don't go making more than there is."

Rufus stared at him. "Next time you wake me. You was supposed to wake me and you didn't. That's what I'm making of it. The breed give any trouble in the night?"

"Not to me," Deakins said.

"He better not give me trouble," Rufus said, rubbing his red streaked eyes. "You hear me, breed? I'll cut your balls off you give me trouble. Ain't nothing I been getting but back talk since this whole thing begun. But there's a cure for that. Yes sir."

Sundance thought Deakins looked edgy.

CHAPTER NINE

Rufus's bad mood got worse as the day went on. Sundance knew it could be just the rotgut whiskey, or he could be working up to something else. Betrayal was most likely. Over the years Rufus had taken no end of abuse from his father. Now the old man had to depend on him, and Rufus was in a position to pay him back for every hard word, every sneer, every curse. It was clear that Rufus's resentment was like a festering wound. The poison was beginning to drip.

Rufus cursed the heat, the mountains, the horses. The food was rotten, the coffee bad. Instead of waiting till they made camp for the night, he tipped a bottle as he rode. But Sundance noticed that he passed it to Leggett and Johnson a few times. None was offered to Deakins, who continued to look edgy in spite of his efforts to look unconcerned.

Sundance wanted to see Deakins dead, but not now. By now he had decided that the dark-faced, little outlaw was the surest way out of this. Deakins had wavered the night before, and he was wavering now. He was the odd man out and he knew it. It showed in his face, in the way he kept abreast of Rufus, never getting ahead of him.

By now they were two days out from the canyon, with about five days to reach Trinidad. Rufus drank enough to be sleepy and said they were going to make an early camp. Leggett and Johnson just shrugged. Men in their late thirties, they were about as intelligent as Rufus. Only Deakins made some protest about the hours of daylight that were being wasted.

"We could push on another six or eight miles," he said, trying to sound reasonable instead of argumentative.

Rufus decided to be offended. "I told you and I told you," he said. "Now I'm going to tell you again. I give the orders here. That town ain't going to blow away on the wind. Another thing. I'm sick of that truck we been eating. Go out there and see if you can shoot something won't make us puke. How many times have I heard you bragging on what a hand you are with a rifle?"

For the first time Deakins looked frightened. The sun still had a long way to go, but he knew he could be caught by darkness. Caught by darkness and with Rufus waiting behind a rock.

"What we got ain't so bad," he wheedled. "Besides we're two days closer to Trinidad."

"They ain't going to hear shooting in Trinidad," Rufus said.

Deakins said, "Use your head, Rufe. There's people closer than Trinidad."

"Not this close," Rufus said. "Ain't nobody this close. What if there is? Ain't no law against shooting your supper. Now take your long gun and go fetch something for the skillet. If you're skeered of a few jack rabbits or gophers, Johnson'll go along and hold your hand. That right, Johnson?"

"Sure thing," Johnson said.

Rufus spat. "Or Leggett. Which one you want?"

Deakins picked up his rifle. "Neither one. I'll get

something if I can.''

"Don't fall down a hole,'' Rufus said.

Sundance waited for Rufus to move out after Deakins, but he stayed where he was, tipping the bottle as he'd been doing all day. He'd been drinking since the moment he opened his eyes and started complaining. But that didn't have to mean so much, Sundance knew. Back-country apes like Rufus drank moonshine before they drank milk, and even as kids, they liked it better. They could rouse up out of their drunkenness when they had to. But still he didn't move.

"That Deakins is an old woman,'' he said to Johnson, who had a little more to say than Leggett.

"I hate old people,'' Johnson said. "Your daddy's the exception to that remark, I hope you know.''

"Don't know any such thing. Have a drink, Johnson,'' Rufus said.

Leggett said, as if the thought had just occurred to him, "I don't mind old people that much. You don't mind me stating the truth, do you, Rufe?''

Rufus grinned at him. "Don't you know it's a free country? You can say what you like. Have a drink, old feller.''

"Thanks,'' Leggett said. "You probably don't like old people so good because they don't smell so good.''

"I don't like how Deakins smells.'' Rufus sniffed and had some difficulty doing it. "Deakins smells like a rat.'' Rufus took a swig of moon and belched before he passed the bottle to the others. "Ever' time I think of that little weasel I get a bad feeling. Then right after the bad feeling comes the rat smell. Something ain't right about that little feller. First time he hooked up with the gang I told Lowry there was something wrong with him.''

Rufus paused to have another drink. Then he went on.

" 'Listen here, you old buzzard,' I says to Lowry, 'What you mean by allowing that little rat's ass to join up with us?' "

Johnson said, "You mean you said that to Lowry?"

"Yeah?" Leggett remarked. "That's strong language to be throwing Lowry's direction."

Rufus was firm. "I said what I said. You mean you don't like the way I'm telling it? Then go find your own bottle."

"Golly Moses!" Johnson put his hand over his heart. "Me and Leggett believes every word you says. Your daddy's a fine man, which don't mean he knows everything there is to know. So what was you saying anyways?"

"About Deakins," Rufus said. "There was the smell of a polecat about that feller, was what I told Lowry. Joins the gang and us men don't know one thing about him. Comes from South Texas, he says, but I'll be damned to the eternal flames of hell if he looks like any South Texas man to me. But like they say, there was nothing I could put my finger on."

Deakins had been gone for about forty-five minutes when a single rifle shot sounded a good distance away. There was a long silence and another shot came. They waited for Deakins to come back, and when he did, he had two jack rabbits, long-eared, dripping with blood. He threw the rabbits by the fire. The rule was when you shot the meat you didn't have to cook it.

"There," Deakins said.

"There what?" Rufus sneered. "You think you're a great big hunter like the Englishman. Get on with the supper, Deakins."

"Let somebody else do that," Deakins said. "I brought it in."

"You do it," Rufus said. "Us fellers like your womanly touch. Roast it just right or we'll send it back to the kitchen. I seen a man that tried to do that in Abilene. The cookie threw the bowl of stew in his face. The old cookie was tough. You ain't."

Deakins looked at Sundance but saw nothing but a blank face. Sundance didn't want any signals passing between them. It was going good, he thought. Rufus was a stupid man, crowding another man when he didn't have to. All he had to do was make a friend of Deakins. After that the killing would be easy.

Leggett and Johnson didn't move.

Now, faced with his own cowardice, Deakins tried to make a joke out of it. "You fellers can't cook anyhow," he said.

"All cooks talk a lot," Rufus said. "For Christ's sake, my stomach's turning over with hunger."

They watched while Deakins skinned the rabbits and skewered the meat on sticks. Soon it hissed over the coals, dripping fat. Rufus shared his whiskey with Leggett and Johnson while the meat cooked.

Deakins got his share of the meat, but it wasn't a fair share. He ate what he got in silence, but Sundance could feel the bitterness in him.

When he finished eating, Rufus wiped his greasy hands on his shirt and sat back with a grin.

"Deakins is going to open a three-stool restaurant when he gets his money," Rufus said. "But he ain't going to prosper at it 'cause all he can fix is burned jack rabbit. Folks in town are going to get sick of that after a while."

Deakins looked up from the fire. "You ate enough of

it. More than enough."

"That's 'cause I'm bigger than you are," Rufus said. "I hate a man doesn't have a sense of humor. That's how come you look so preacher-faced all the time. You'd like to have a good time, but you can't."

"There's no call for all this," Deakins said. "I pull my weight like every other man."

Rufus winked at the others. "Golly gee, I didn't know you was so thin-skinned. Come on now, boy. You're part of the family, ain't you? Wouldn't josh you so hard if I didn't feel for you like my own brother. Let's see a smile there, Brother Deakins. Hell! You don't know when a feller is funning and when he ain't."

"I can take a joke." Deakins made an attempt to smile. "It's just that I get sick of it. You know how it goes?"

Rufus yawned. "'Deed I do. No hard feelings now?"

Leggett and Johnson took the first two watches and it was well past midnight when Deakins picked up his rifle and took over. Sundance knew he hadn't been asleep. He could see the lines of fatigue in Deakins's face when he built up the fire, shivering against the mountain cold. The fire crackled as the wind blew harder. The moon had faded.

Sundance was facing the fire, his hands secured behind him. This time Deakins sat closer after making sure that Rufus was asleep. The hobbled horses moved about.

"He's working himself up to kill you," Sundance said. "He's working up to stealing the money. Only the thought of his father is keeping him from it."

Deakins rubbed his face and told Sundance to shut up. "I don't trust you no more than him. I know him better than you."

The wind blew wood ash from the edge of the fire.

"You'll be dead if you don't make up your mind, Deakins. That business with the rabbits, that's only the start of it. Next time he'll say you're talking back and kill you. They'll all throw down on you. Why do you think he's been feeding them whiskey? Why do you think he sent you out of camp? They were talking after you left."

Deakins stared with dead eyes. "Now you're going to tell me what they said?"

"Can't do that. They moved away from me so I couldn't hear. But I can tell when men are planning something. Don't tell me you wanted to go out there?"

Deakins didn't answer.

Sundance said, "I thought you were a goner for sure."

"You'd be a goner too."

"Not as fast as you would," Sundance said. "What's the matter with you? You'll keep hemming and hawing till they cut loose with bullets. You can't take on the three of them, not while they're awake. Do it now."

Sweat glistened on Deakins's face. Indecision quivered inside him like jelly. "Leave me alone," he said.

"Can't leave you alone," Sundance went on. "You're going to get us killed. Face up to it. Throw in with me. How much worse off can you be? Rufus is a maniac and you know it."

"I seen him like this before."

"Not when there was a hundred thousand on the table. What can you lose by siding with me?"

"Maybe nothing," Deakins said. "I just got to figure it out."

"What's there to figure?" Sundance said. "You have the gun and there they are, sleeping. Kill Rufus first, then the others. They're so close. How can you miss?"

"You're asking me to kill who I rode with?"

"Don't be dumb. They don't think the same about you. Look at the truth, Deakins. You don't give a damn about them. There must be some way to make you see what you're up against. No matter which way you turn, you're going to get killed."

"Shut up, I'm telling you." Deakin's voice was unsteady and he kept moving his left shoulder. It was the same as a twitch in another man's face. "I'll use a gun barrel on your head, I'm warning you."

"That's very smart, Deakins."

Sundance closed his eyes, feigning sleep.

He listened while Deakins fidgeted by the fire. There was the rattle of a cup and the sound of coffee being poured. After that it was quiet. Sundance slept because there was nothing else to be said to Deakins. The little bastard had to be needled, but it couldn't all be done at one time. But the time was getting close now. In another twenty-four hours they would be only two days from Trinidad. If they got that far, there was no telling what would happen. Deakins might yet decide to take his chances with Rufus.

Sundance opened his eyes when he heard Deakins telling Rufus it was time to stand his watch. There was mumbling followed by a loud curse.

"You're up, ain't you, Deakins?" Rufus said. "Go to hell. I got to get my sleep. You wake me again and you'll be sorry for it."

Muttering to himself Deakins came back to the fire. Sundance didn't try any more persuading; best to let Deakins stew a little longer. But if nothing happened by the following night he would have to make some kind of move before they tied him up for the night. Best time would be suppertime, when they were tired and thinking of nothing but food.

In a change of mood, Rufus said nothing to Deakins in the morning. He just didn't look at him all through the day. To Sundance it was certain that Rufus had made up his mind about the killing and the money. Leggett and Johnson were just as doomed as Deakins, but they didn't know it. But Deakins knew it. At least he sensed it. His movements were quick and nervous. He tensed at the slightest sound, and the more he tried to calm himself, the jumpier he got.

If Rufus noticed this he had nothing to say about it. Even the sneering jokes had dried up. Sundance guessed Deakins was sorry he hadn't taken his offer. Now, in bright sunlight, there was no chance to do anything that would work. Deakins had a pistol and a saddle gun, but he couldn't throw one or the other to Sundance without getting killed. Sundance didn't know how well Leggett and Johnson could handle a gun, but the old man said he was sending his best men. He spat when he said it, but Sundance guessed they were good enough. He guessed Leggett would be a little better than Johnson. It made no difference if Rufus decided to kill Deakins before night fell.

They made camp by a tree that had been blasted by lightning. Deakins started to gather wood, but Rufus said Johnson would do it. Johnson didn't say anything. Deakins said, "The wood is just laying there, Rufe."

Rufus didn't look at him. "You been working enough, Deak. Why don't you take a drink?" Rufus held up a bottle. "Stuff's four days old by now. I'd call that well aged for moon."

"Obliged to you," Deakins said. "But my gut's been a little bit off the last week. Think I'll stick with the coffee."

Rufus took a short drink. "Got a pain in the belly,

have you, Deak? You ain't going to get sick or nothing like that?"

"Something I et. You know me, Rufe. Thing as small as a bellyache ain't going to lay me low. I'm a tough old buzzard from way back."

"That you are, Deak," Rufus agreed.

Rufus tipped the bottle a lot but swallowed very little, though he smacked his lips as if he'd downed a real snorter. He's going to kill Deakins tonight, Sundance thought. That's why he's going slow with the bottle, making sure his aim won't be off. Sundance was sure that Rufus wouldn't try to kill Leggett and Johnson at the same time. Rufus might have been fast enough to do it, but he wouldn't take that much of a chance.

They ate and Deakins tied Sundance for the night while the others watched. Deakins pulled hard on the ropes and turned Sundance so the loose knots wouldn't show. There was no moon and the only light came from the fire. For a moment Rufus seemed ready to make his move, but he turned aside yawning. Deakins had picked up his rifle a little too fast.

"I'll take the first watch," Deakins said, holding the rifle in one hand, his trigger finger resting outside the trigger guard.

"Anything you like, Deak," Rufus said. "I ain't sleepy so I'll just sit awhile and have a few more drinks. You boys get your sleep."

The dead tree threw spiky shadows on the rocks behind it. Sparks from the fire went up into the darkness. A horse whinnied and that was all. Rufus tilted the bottle and yawned. A few minutes later he closed his eyes.

Sundance, putting pressure on the ropes, knew that Rufus wasn't asleep. It could come any minute. Seconds before he freed his hands. Maybe Leggett and Johnson were asleep. No way to tell. His roped hands were facing away from Rufus, but too much movement would betray him. Slowly, his wrists barely moving, the ropes came loose. Deakins got up to put more wood on the fire, still holding the rifle in his right hand. For a moment he turned to look at Sundance. Sundance, out of Rufus's line of sight, nodded. His hands were free now, but there was nothing he could do about his legs. He would have to shoot from where he was. But there was still a chance. Deakins whirled and threw his belt gun to Sundance and fired at Rufus and missed. Sundance caught the pistol in midair as Rufus came up shooting. Sundance shot Rufus twice in the chest and he went down. Deakins jumped away from the fire and shot at Leggett and Johnson. A bullet caught Deakins in the shoulder and spun him around. He stumbled and fell as Sundance used up five shots on Leggett and Johnson. They dropped and Sundance turned his gun on Deakins, who was grabbing for his dropped rifle. His hand was on the stock when Sundance put a bullet in the back of his head.

There wasn't a sound as Sundance untied the ropes that bound his ankles. No one moved. They were dead. They lay in the grotesque attitudes of death while the wind plucked at their hair. Rufus's face looked better than it had in life. The snarl that marked him in life was gone. The horses had moved away from the camp, frightened by the sudden burst of gunfire. But hobbled as they were, they hadn't gone far.

Collecting the guns and ammunition, Sundance knew the camp wasn't far from where Eagle had been turned loose. Or so Manning said. There wasn't much time left. Still it was worth a try. The loss of the big stallion hadn't preyed on his mind, though he had thought about it at times. He was as unsentimental about animals as he was about people. But the big-blooded horse would make all the difference in the fight that was to come.

He dragged Deakins's body away from the fire and put it with the others. He felt no remorse. The dark-faced little man had been an outlaw—a killer—like the others. To Sundance his death meant no more than the killing of a snake. He pulled his long-barreled Colt from Rufus's belt and checked the firing pin. It was gone. Sundance smiled, thinking of the old man's foxiness. A firing pin could be replaced in minutes. It didn't matter. He had four Winchesters and four pistols, plenty of ammunition, still plenty of water, and when he got to the creek he would have more. He found a knife in Rufus's boot.

The night he slept by the fire. The bodies lying in the brush didn't bother him. During the night coyotes came prowling, drawn by the smell of human carrion, and he didn't mind that either. After he boiled coffee he checked what he needed to get the Mannings out.

He needed ropes to get down the steep canyon wall. There was plenty of rope. There were five horses; six if he found Eagle. He didn't think there was the smallest chance of killing all of Lowry's men. They'd be lucky if they managed to escape. If they got out they'd be in for a chase, maybe a long one, for the old man wouldn't give up. When he came after them he'd come with blood in his eye. A long chase would require plenty of water. The whole thing might be decided by water. What the old man would do was try to corner them until their water gave out. That wouldn't take so long. Then the old man would move in, ready to deal out death by inches.

Sundance led the string of horses away from camp and headed for the creek. An hour later he saw it from the top of a ridge. It flowed between cottonwoods and alders, bright in the morning sun. The horses whinnied when they smelled the fresh water, and it took some doing to hold them in check. Down from the ridge, he hobbled the horses and let them drink. Along the creek there was good grass and the horses would stay without being watched. He followed the creek downstream, knowing that Eagle would go to deep water. There were signs that the grass had been cropped, but that didn't mean that Eagle was close by. Wild burros were all over these mountains. He waded into the water. At first there was nothing but sand. Then he came to a rocky place and his heart quickened when he picked up a smooth stone and saw the scratches on it. They were faint but they were there. Only a shod horse could have marked the stone that way.

Moving on he found other stones nicked and scratched. He was inspecting another stone when he heard Eagle whinny far downstream and then he heard the thunder of the stallion hoofs coming toward him. In a few minutes he saw the great horse that had served him so well in so many places. The big horse stopped and approached shyly at Sundance's command.

"Good boy," Sundance said while Eagle nuzzled his chest.

Grass and water had kept the stallion in good condition. The saddle was gone, but that didn't matter a damn. He vaulted onto Eagle's back and felt all his confidence return. Let the bastards try to stop me now, he thought. He had lost all his weapons except for the long-barreled Colt. That didn't matter either. Not many days before he had been inches from death. Now he had his horse and he was coming back to rescue the man who had tried to kill him.

He would give Edward Manning his life and, having given it, he would take it away. That was the deal. He hadn't talked it over with Manning. There had been no need.

The other horses were spread out along the creek and now he had to approach them cautiously. The presence of the big fighting horse made them nervous. He spoke quietly to the animals, letting them know there was no danger. Eagle kept his distance as he had been trained to do, while Sundance rinsed out the canteens and filled them, stoppering them securely. Then he took the saddle from Rufus's horse and put it on Eagle. It was time to start back.

Buzzards were squawking in the brush where the dead men lay. Four down, Sundance thought. Well watered and grassed, the string of horses moved at a good clip, giving no trouble. He had been over this country twice in as many weeks. There was no longer any hesitation, no need to look for a trail. If anything, the trail was beginning to be too well marked by campfires and, Sundance smiled, the bodies of men.

He rested the horses and moved on. Eagle moved without effort, but the other horses didn't have the big stallion's strength and had to be rested. He gave them water when they needed it. A bunch of wild burros broke from cover and ran away, braying and kicking up their heels. He saw other animals but no men sent by Lowry to watch for his money. That didn't mean they weren't there, watching over rifle barrels, for there was constant danger in dealing with a man like Lowry.

Night came but there was a moon and he moved on, always watching for an ambush. When he decided the horses had traveled enough for one day, he hobbled them and made cold camp, no fire. It was cold and windy and he thought of the coffee he didn't have.

He lay awake thinking of how he was going to do it. The mouth of the dead-end canyon was guarded by two men at all times. The old man slept by himself in the stone house, the rest of them out in the open under tarpaulins. The back wall of the canyon, not far from where the Mannings were, was sheer rock about two hundred feet high. It wasn't guarded and that was where he would come down. The guns would have to be lowered first, after they were wrapped in a blanket and tied so they wouldn't rattle. Then he would come down himself. The corral was between the spring and the back wall of the canyon. If the horses spooked before he got to the bottom they could kill him at their leisure. With enough of them shooting at him, there was no way they could miss.

He knew he was going to have to depend on Manning to get it done. The brother might hold up under fire, but he didn't know much, if anything, about killing men. He didn't know how the woman would take it. When the shooting started she might freeze up or run the wrong way.

Eagle and the rest of the horses would have to be left a fair distance from the canyon. There was a place that looked all right. He would leave them there. He wondered if he could get as far as the house in the dark. If he could kill the old man, the others would be without a leader for a while. But it was too far to the house, he decided, too much ground to cover. Besides, there was no guarantee that the old man would be there. Doing the unpredictable was what had kept him alive for so long. No, the men guarding the Mannings had to be the first to die. There had been two men. There might still

135

be two men if the old man hadn't changed things. There was a chance that he had moved the Mannings to another place.

Wait and see, Sundance thought, and went to sleep.

He started again before dawn and by the end of the next day he had reached the edge of the desert. After watering the horses, he crossed it in one night and part of a day. Baptiste's body was bones when he came up out of the desert and started on the last lap of the journey.

From now on he would have to watch himself all the time.

CHAPTER TEN

Now there were less than five miles to go and Sundance walked the horses because their dust might be spotted by lookouts if he pushed them any faster. Earlier he hobbled the horses and left them in a draw while he went ahead mounted on Eagle. He circled out far and came in from the other side, searching for bushwhackers. After searching for an hour he went back to the horses and waited for night to come. He watered the horses and let them graze on what they could find.

While he waited he checked the weapons he had taken from the dead men. All were well cared for. He laid them in a blanket after loading, then he coiled the gunbelts and put them in too. Last to be bundled up were the canteens that had been emptied on the way back. When he had tied the load he hefted it and found it all right.

The sun dropped away to the west, washing everything in red. The shadows grew longer and he waited for another thirty minutes. They wouldn't be able to see him now, even if they were using binoculars. The horses were quiet and well behaved, subdued by the stallion's presence. He led them from the draw, walking them, one roped to the other, starting out on what might be the last night of his life. The sky changed color and a pale moon showed without giving much light. As he led the horses he kept to sand as much as possible, stopping now and then to listen. There was nothing but the wind, now growing cold.

He knew the two lookouts were posted on both sides of the canyon mouth, high up and well concealed. When he broke out with the horses from the corral they would be under fire. There was nothing to be done about the two lookouts. It was too risky. One shot, one yell would wake up the whole gang and maybe get the Mannings killed.

He left the horses in the place he had decided on earlier. It was about a mile from the canyon, a circle of rocks with only one way in. "Hold them here, boy," he told Eagle. Then he went on by himself, carrying the ropes and the bundle of weapons. The knife he had taken from Rufus's body was stuck inside his belt. It had a thumb guard and a long haft with copper rivets.

The moon was brighter as he moved around to the west wall of the canyon. There were no sounds, not even the whirring wings of night birds. The west wall of the canyon sloped up high and was covered with dense brush. He moved a few steps at a time, feeling for holes that might trip him. In places he had to turn back and start again in order to find a way through the brush. It took a long time to reach the back wall of the canyon.

High on the rock he could see down into the canyon. There was light in the house and that meant the old man was still up and around. He waited without impatience, and after an hour the light went out. By then he had the first rope secured to a rock and he put all his weight on it. It held fast and he joined the second rope and tested that too. When he was satisfied that it would hold him, he coiled it and put it down.

Clouds drifted across the moon as he tied another rope to the bundle of weapons. He made two loops and joined them in the middle so that there would be balance. Down in the canyon a match flared and went out. The light came from over by the spring, so it looked like the Mannings hadn't been moved to another place. He started to lower the weapons to the bottom. There was a place where the rock bulged out, and unless he did it right the bundle of weapons would swing inward and bang against the cliff. Inch by inch he paid out the rope. The wind gusted up and he felt the sudden swing of the rope. There was nothing he could do but wait for the wind to ease up. It seemed like hours before he felt the rope slacken and knew the weapons were safely at the bottom. Only then did he release the rope. It fell without a sound.

Before he began his descent he wedged the belt gun tight in its holster. He went down and at times his feet touched the rock, but after he went over the bulge in the rock he was hanging free, with no support other than the rope. Halfway down he thought he heard voices, but couldn't be sure because of the noise of the bubbling sounds of the spring as it splashed over the rocks. This was the worst part, the halfway point. If they started shooting now he'd be killed if he clung to the rope, killed if he dropped because there was still a hundred feet to go. Finally his feet touched ground and he was in the deep shadow of the cliff.

His hands were raw and stiff from the rope. He clenched and unclenched them to get the blood flowing again. In the corral the horses moved around and one of them let out a loud whinny that threatened to turn into loud panic. The two guards called back and forth until the horses settled down.

Moving from rock to rock he carried the bundle of weapons until it was dangerous to bring it any closer. He put it down and cut the ropes that held it together and left it as it was until he was sure the guards hadn't moved. Then he moved on, a shadow among shadows. A match flared again as a guard lit another cigarette. Sundance could see the man who was smoking, a squat shape on a rock, a rifle across his knees. He couldn't see the second man and could only guess where he was.

Holding the knife, Sundance went down on his belly in the grass and began to crawl toward the first man he had to kill. Smoke from the cigarette drifted in the moonlight. The squat shape on the rock became the outline of a man as he crawled closer. The moon clouded over and reappeared. Sundance looked up at the sky, waiting for clouds to move in again. It would have to be done in darkness, or the second guard might spot the attack and open fire. The killing would have to be done not only in darkness but in silence. A hand clamped over the mouth, an upward thrust under the ribcage. Death was instantaneous if the blade penetrated the heart on the first stroke. Then the body had to be lowered to the ground, all without a sound.

Now he was directly behind the man on the rock; so close that he could smell the man's sweat, hear the wheezing sound his lungs made as they sucked in cigarette smoke.

As the clouds moved in so did the shadows. The moonlight faded to blackness and Sundance raised up fast and killed the man. He was halfway to where he figured the other guard was before the pale light came back and flooded the canyon. He stopped when the guard stood up and stretched and went to the spring with his rifle in one hand.

"Don't get nervous, Shack," he called out. "It's just me going to get a drink."

. The guard was lying on his belly by the spring when Sundance shoved his head under water and buried the knife in his back. He struggled for a moment before he died. Bubbles floated to the surface after he was dead. Edward Manning stepped from the shadow of the cliff and Sundance put the knife away.

"I saw you coming down the cliff," Manning said. "I've been watching for hours."

"Get the others," Sundance whispered back. "The horses are moving around too much. Tell the others they'll be riding bareback. Tell them to hang on and stay low. We'll be going out through heavy fire."

Sundance was passing out the guns when a light came on in the house. Alison Manning jerked with fright and Sundance clapped his hand over her mouth. The light in the house stayed on.

"We have to go now," Sundance whispered. "Move into the corral and get your wife mounted up. I'll open the gate when you're ready to ride."

Manning didn't move and his voice was calm, almost matter of fact. "I'd like to get my rifle. The old man has it. What's to stop me from getting it?"

Sundance dug his pistol into Manning's belly. "I'll stop you. You may see enough of your rifle before this is over."

Holding the gate Sundance watched them mount up. The horse Alison Manning was on kept circling, not trying to throw her, but nervous. Sundance eased open the gate and the horses in the corral went wild, kicking at the rails, all trying to get out at the same time. Immediately there was shouting from all directions and the door of the house banged open. As the Mannings swept past him, carried along by the stampeded, Sundance vaulted onto the back of a running horse. Flashes of fire came at them from the darkness and there was shooting from the front of the house. Sundance heard the old man yelling louder than the others. Up ahead Manning was returning the fire of the men who were trying to turn back the horses. A shape sprang at Sundance and tried to bring him down. He shot the man in the face and he went down under the hoofs of the horses behind.

Gunfire chased them to the end of the canyon. Before they got that far the two lookouts had opened fire. The horses in the lead were pouring out through the mouth of the canyon. Sundance fired at a flash high on a rock and saw a shape falling to the ground. Someone else fired. Manning? The other lookout came crashing down. The gunfire faded as they left the canyon behind.

Two hundred yards out Sundance found Alison Manning staggering blindly. She tried to run when she heard him coming. He ran the horse behind her and scooped her up in front of him. "No! No!" she cried out. "William has been wounded. He's lying there somewhere. We have to go back. Where's Edward?"

Manning had turned his horse and came galloping back. "Your brother's been hit, we have to find him," Sundance said.

"That wasn't what you said when you planned this," Manning said.

"I changed my mind," Sundance said. "You can run if you like. You won't get far without a bridle. Go on, Manning, run."

Holding the woman in front of him, Sundance started back. Manning rode after him. In the darkness they found William Manning lying on the ground with a bullet wound in his shoulder. He was unconscious and he groaned when Sundance shook him awake, then lifted him and put him on his brother's horse.

"Hold onto him," Sundance said. "The fall knocked him out. You let him fall off and I'll kill you."

"So you say," Manning said calmly. "They'll be rounding up the horses before long."

"That won't be so easy in the dark," Sundance said. "But the old man will be along. You can bet on that. He won't give up till he's dead, or we are. How does it feel to be hunted for a change?"

Manning turned his horse. "It will be a new experience," he said. "Hang on, old man," he said to his brother. "There's a chance we may all get back to England."

Not you, Sundance thought.

With the horses carrying double it took them a long time to get back to where Eagle was. The stallion whinnied when he saw Sundance.

"See, I didn't kill your horse," Manning said.

Sundance told him to shut up. He took William Manning down from the horse and sat him against a rock and slit his shirt open. There was blood on the back of his shirt. The bullet had gone through without doing any serious damage.

"There's not much we can do about it now," Sundance said to Manning's wife. "Bind it up as fast you can. It won't be long before the old man is ready to move."

"You think we'll make it back to Trinidad?" Manning asked. Now that he was free he was ready to be cocky again. "A pity about William. He's going to slow us up."

Sundance said, "We're not going to Trinidad. We're going over the mountains to Santa Fe. New Mexico is closer and the old man may not want to hunt us deep into a territory where the law is eager to hang him. That's just a hope. I don't know what he'll do. Anyway, he'll hunt us hard. We have to find a way to kill him."

"I wish I had my rifle," Manning said. "The old man wouldn't even get close if I had my rifle."

"The old man has your rifle," Sundance said. "He doesn't have to get close. He won't be half as sporting as you were with me."

Manning spoke as if he hadn't understood the bitterness in Sundance's voice. "That's true," he said. "I could have killed you any number of times."

"You should have; now it's too late."

Manning smiled. "We'll see about that," he said.

William Manning was able to sit a horse, and not much else: Alison Manning was to stay close to him, to see that he didn't topple from the saddle. Her husband led the three riderless horses. They started out in darkness.

Sundance wasn't sure that William Manning would come out of the fog that had been caused by the fall. The shoulder wound wasn't so bad; concussion could do a lot more damage. The man needed rest and that was something he couldn't have.

Sundance was thinking about the damned Weatherby bolt-action, now in Lowry's capable hands. It was the old man's artillery. It might take him a while to get used to the big rifle, but once he did they could expect the worst. He would use it on the horses, on the woman, if he could.

Santa Fe lay dead south, beyond the mountains, and

they had enough water to get there if Lowry didn't force them into a siege. Dawn glimmered to full light as they rode toward the mountains that separated them from safety. Along about now Lowry and what was left of his gang would be mounting up for the chase. If it hadn't been for William Manning they could have outrun the old man. The original plan called for the abandonment of the wounded, yet Sundance knew he wasn't going to leave William Manning if for no other reason than it would serve his brother too well.

Alison Manning had given up all pretense. She ignored her husband as she cared for his brother. When William Manning swayed in the saddle, she rode up close and steadied him, speaking quiet words of encouragement.

They stopped to give the horses water and rest. Manning's wife helped his brother from the saddle and held the canteen while he drank. Manning seemed to find it amusing.

Sundance climbed down from a high rock and Manning walked over to him. "There's something I must ask you," he said. "Did you ever think of sending for the money and taking it yourself?"

Sundance told him to go to hell.

Manning just laughed. "It's just as well you didn't. There was no hundred thousand. But it got us out, didn't it?"

Sundance knocked him down with a left to the belly, a right to the jaw. Then he drew his gun and cocked it. Manning lay in the dust spitting blood.

Sundance held the gun steady and pretended to be angrier than he was. "You came close that time, Manning. Every time you open your mouth you get closer."

Manning wasn't smiling now. "You wouldn't care to

145

try that without the gun?''

Sundance holstered his gun. "Get up, you stupid bastard. I don't think you even know what's real." He didn't care if he had to kill Manning in front of his wife. Not now. She'd be better off without him. So would the world.

The water would last them for a time, but there was no food. Sundance could have killed meat on the way back. Without salt it would be bad by now. If push came to shove, he would kill one of the horses.

Sundance turned when Manning's wife cried out. "William won't open his eyes. He closed his eyes, just for a minute to rest, and he won't wake up. Can't you do something?''

"Perhaps he's dead," Manning said, amused again.

"You rotten bastard," his wife screamed.

"Quit it," Sundance ordered, pushing her aside. He felt William Manning's pulse and put his ear to his chest. The heartbeat was light and rapid.

Alison Manning's face was drawn with worry. "Is he going to be all right?''

"He took a knock in the head, he's been riding in the sun. I don't know. Pour water on his face, slap him a few times. We can't stay here.''

William Manning groaned but didn't respond. "Let me see what I can do," Sundance said, pinching the big nerve on the inside of the unconscious man's thigh. He opened his eyes in pain and confusion.

Sundance shook him. "Are you able to travel? You passed out. Heat. Concussion. Something. You understand what I'm saying? We have to move on.''

"Move on? Yes, of course. The bandits.''

Sundance gave him more water and lifted him onto his horse. Then he roped his ankles under the horse and tied his wrists to the saddle horn.

"At least he won't fall off," Manning said, swinging into the saddle with the ease of a born horseman. "The way we're going, we might as well walk to New Mexico."

Sundance hated Manning's guts, but he was right. They were fast losing the time they needed. So far there were no signs of pursuit. That would come all too soon. If William Manning just up and died it would make everything that much simpler. The hell of it was that he might die anyway; no one knew that much about head injuries, not even the doctors. But he'd be damned if he'd hasten the man's death. Like the Indians said, when you saved a man's life you had to take good care of it.

After an hour in the saddle William Manning blacked out again, and he would have crashed to the ground if the ropes hadn't held him in place. As it was, he lurched from side to side like a sack of meal. His hat fell off and Sundance scooped it up from the dust and jammed it back on his head.

Manning, seeing how Sundance did it, nodded appreciatively. "You picked it up right from the saddle. I must learn to do that."

Alison Manning turned an agonized face to Sundance. "You're killing him. We have to stop. Go on if you like. I'll stay with him."

"You want to be roped too?" Sundance meant it. "All right. Then see that he stays on his horse. We're going as easy as we can. He'll be better off with us than with Lowry. It won't be so bad after the sun is down."

"That will be hours from now."

"No help for it. Keep him moving."

When the day ended they had gone only half the dis-

147

tance Sundance had counted on. Through all the long day there hadn't been a trace of water. Manning turned his horse and rode back. He had taken the Morgan, the biggest horse in the bunch, but it was a docile animal and not half as spirited as he wanted it to be.

"How's the patient?" he said, fingering the bruise on his chin without meaning too. He jerked his hand away.

"I don't know," Sundance said. "I'm not going to leave him, so don't start on that again."

Manning said calmly, "It would be the sensible thing to do."

"I hit you once, Manning. I can do it again any time I like."

"Can you now? I wouldn't advise it." Manning's hand reached for his gun, but it wasn't even close before he found himself staring into the cocked pistol Sundance held on him. Suddenly he smiled. "I must learn how to do that too. We were talking about my brother. I was told you served in the Union Army, but I see it didn't take, as we say."

"We didn't leave our wounded in the Union Army. The Rebs didn't either." Sundance knew he wasn't going to kill Manning for running off at the mouth. The pistol didn't scare him. What did scare him? Maybe nothing. He put the gun away.

"But sometimes you shot the wounded, didn't you?" Manning said. "We did that in the Sudan. It had to be done."

"Not here, Manning. If there's any shooting here I'll do it. There won't be. Stay away from your brother, I'm telling you."

Manning stood still. "It's your show. As you say, you'll have to kill him. Go on, draw your gun again. You think that changes what has to be done? You think

148

I say he should be shot because I want to save my life?"

"You said you could raise a hundred thousand, Manning. You were ready to set me up against a marked deck."

"I gambled that it wouldn't get that far. I was right." Manning smiled. "Or did you call my bluff?"

"Maybe." Sundance decided to do some bluffing himself. "The old man started with fifty thousand, He never stole that much from all the robberies in a long life. Then he doubled the money. A hundred thousand. You said all right without blinking an eye. You'd have said all right if he asked for a million."

"Ah, I see," Manning said.

"Or ten million," Sundance said.

Manning smiled. "What's the difference? It wasn't a lie. I don't lie and I think you know it. A diversionary tactic, is how I see it. Necessary at the moment."

"Like killing your brother."

"Oh, don't worry. He can't hear us and my dear wife isn't listening. I'm not afraid to die, but I don't want to die because you won't stick to the rules. If I were in William's place I'd tell you to shoot me. I'd order you."

"Your days of giving orders are over, Manning. And your goddamned schoolboy rules don't apply here. You should have stayed at home where you could risk your life in a safe way. It doesn't work here."

"Then your decision is no," Manning said. "I'm disappointed in you, Sundance. You're not at all the sort of man I thought you were. For all the things you've done, you're just like the rest of them."

Sundance thought of all the decent people he had known in his life. Ordinary people. The sort of people Manning despised. He thought of a drunken, illiterate, mumbling old black man who had saved him from a hang mob in the Indian Territory. He thought of a little Indian girl who had kept him from being burned alive by killers who wanted to take what he was protecting.

And others.

"I hope I'm like the rest of them," he said to Manning. "Just so I'm nothing like you."

CHAPTER ELEVEN

Only minutes of light were left when Sundance climbed
the rock. He was close to the top when a bullet blew
rock splinters in his face. He knew the sound and knew
the scope was moving toward him for a second shot. He
rolled off the rock, falling as it seemed in a tangle of
arms and legs. He was on his feet when he hit the
ground. Manning looked at him and stoppered the canteen he was drinking from. The Weatherby didn't fire
again.

"He started before the others," Manning said calmly.
"By himself or with just a few men. He didn't wait to
round up all the horses. What now, Commander?"

Manning's wife had pulled his brother to the ground
and was protecting him with her body. She was shaking.

"The one he's after is me," Sundance said. No more
shots came. "He'll be after me all the time. He may have
a few men, he may be on his own. You want to climb up
and draw fire?"

"I know how good my rifle is," Manning said. "It'll
be dark in a minute. The scope's no good then. As if
you didn't know. You want to know how many rounds
he took away from me? Fifty. They're big ones and you
can't carry so many."

Manning seemed to be enjoying himself, the son of a

151

bitch. The sky was dark red like blood that had been spilled and dried. Away to the west there was a crack of thunder. It rolled away as the sky pressed down. It began to rain. Manning, lying beside Sundance, took off his hat and held his face up to the rain. The rain was turning the dust to mud that would be dry an hour after the rain stopped. The sides of the wet horses shone in the last of the light. Thunder rolled again.

Manning said, "He won't be able to see much now. But then neither will we."

Sundance was trying to figure out where the old man was. The bullet had come from the left, but he wouldn't be there now. Ten yards away, maybe a hundred. The old bandit's dream of a comfortable retirement had been wrecked. Add a hangover to that and there was one mean man at the other end of that rifle. The rifle bolted one round at a time, but it bolted them fast.

Manning had a Winchester carbine and he didn't like it. But he was smiling. Sundance could see his teeth, very white in the dark. "What now, Commander?" he repeated.

The rain was letting up as the clouds and the thunder rolled away. Sundance, keeping low, went over to Alison Manning, still trembling and white-faced.

"What's going to happen?" she said. "You said they wouldn't be here so soon."

"Maybe just the old man," Sundance said. "We have to get out of here. How is he?"

"He's alive but you can't make him go on. You'll have to leave us. Maybe I can hold them off for a while."

Sundance yanked her to her feet. "We're not dead yet, so don't be so heroic. I didn't go to all this trouble to abandon you to that scum. Do what I tell you or I'll slap you silly. Your friend goes on his horse, alive or dead."

"You're a strange man, Sundance."

Sundance smiled. "To get mixed up with people like you I must be."

Alison Manning threw her arms around him and he pushed her away. Her husband came close. He said, "I feel left out." He raised his hands in mock distress. "No more fisticuffs—please."

A bullet took away the top of his ear and he was still standing when Sundance hooked his foot under his ankle and brought him down. He lay bleeding in the dust.

"That was close," he said. He smiled his crazy smile.

They got William Manning on his horse and Sundance stayed behind to face the old man's rifle. No other guns had fired. That could be a trick. Lowry was full of tricks. There might be some men with him. He might be by himself.

"You think there's any chance of catching him in a crossfire?" Manning said, ignoring the blood that dripped on his shirt.

"We don't know where he is. He won't be where he shot from. We better move on and try to get him in the morning. If we don't, he's going to get lucky with that rifle."

Manning smiled. "He doesn't need to get lucky, not with my Weatherby. Are you sorry you came back?"

"Not as long as you're alive. Save the talk and move on. I'll catch up to you."

It was dark now and Sundance waited for the sound of the horses to die away, and when he could no longer hear them he moved out to face the big rifle. He circled, crawling when there was no cover. Nothing happened.

After a while he saw the dull glint of an empty cartridge casing, but there was no sign of the old man. Chances were that he had left his horse a long way back, then came ahead on foot. So far it looked like the old man was on his own, but it couldn't be long before the rest of the gang showed up.

He overtook the Mannings about three miles from where they started. "He playing it foxy," Sundance said. "I guess he figures there's no hurry."

Manning said, "Why should he hurry at the rate we're moving? We'll have to make a fight of it sooner or later."

"Then let it be later. The others in the gang may drop off. They're all wanted in New Mexico and won't be that ready to hang."

"You have no real plan of action?"

"Not till I find out how many men he has. That can't be done before daylight. I don't think they'll take us on in the dark. All we can do now is find a place to hole up for the night."

They found a scatter of rocks that could be defended. William Manning was mumbling when they took him off the horse and covered him with a blanket. There was nothing to eat, but no one said anything about it. Alison Manning dropped off to sleep.

"You better do the same," Sundance told Manning. "I'll take the first watch."

"I'll watch with you," Manning said. "You may be wrong in thinking they won't attack us by night."

"Suit yourself," Sundance said. "I'm just guessing they won't attack in the dark. They don't even know where we are. Besides, we have a good position here."

Manning said, "You could easily get away on that stallion of yours. You got us out. You did the best you could. There's no sense in us all dying."

"One of us is going to die," Sundance said. "I'm going to save your wife and brother so they can have some kind of life without you. You won't be going back to England. You won't be going anywhere. The only reason you're still alive is I need your rifle when the shooting starts."

"And if we do get out, what then? How do you intend to kill me? Will you hunt me the way I hunted you? I'm not much good at making bows and arrows."

"You'll get a better chance than you gave me. It will be a fair fight all the way. It's more than you deserve, but I won't gun you down like a dog."

"You may not kill me at all," Manning said. "My rifle is ready to fire right now. Is yours?"

"It's ready," Sundance answered. "Try it if you like."

"Under the circumstances that would be unwise," Manning said calmly. "But you 'mustn't think that killing me is going to be easy. I've lived hard and I'll die the same way. If you want my opinion, I think you're something of a fool. You're risking your life for nothing at all."

"It's my life, Manning."

"It may not be for much longer. That's not a threat, simply a statement of fact. I can't let you kill me, Sundance, but you must believe I feel no animosity toward you. Never have. In many ways you're the most remarkable man I've ever met. Now I'm going to sleep for a while. Goodnight."

During the night Sundance thought he heard sounds carried on the wind. Then the wind changed and he heard nothing for the rest of his watch. Manning awoke the instant Sundance tapped him on the boot with the muzzle of his rifle.

"You think you heard them?" he said.

"I heard something," Sundance said. "A long way off. We'll pull out of here in two hours. But we'll have to make better time tomorrow. The way we're going is no good. The old man must be wondering what's taking us so long. If he finds out something is wrong he'll get bolder."

In the morning, William Manning was awake and able to talk. Sundance looked at the wound and said it didn't look too bad. If it didn't fester in the next twenty-four hours he might be all right.

"You'll have to hang on as best you can," he said. "How's your head? Don't say it's all right if it isn't."

"I'm very dizzy, that's all. But I think I'll be able to ride."

"You'd better," Sundance said.

They rode out before first light, heading deeper into the mountains. The morning sky was streaked with red and it was cold until the sun came up. There was no need to tie William Manning to the saddlehorn; he sat his horse well enough. The horses were using up the water, but there was nothing to be done about that. Without the horses they were as good as dead.

"You'd think the old man would give it up," Manning said. "That's what a reasonable man would do."

"Lowry isn't feeling reasonable. He may have hated his son, but that won't count now. Half his gang is wiped out. He won't give up."

Manning said, "Isn't there any way we can lose our trail?"

"Not a chance. He's been hunted all his life, so he knows how to hunt other men."

"You know we'll have to fight if he's that persistent."

"When the time comes we will. Right now I'm going to check our back trail."

He climbed a rock higher than the others, and thinking of the long range rifle, he went up on the safe side. Lying there he could see back for miles. At first there was nothing, then he saw them coming fast. They came up out of a draw and got closer while he watched. Now he was able to make our four men and four horses, but the distance was still too great to tell them apart. He didn't have to guess that one of them was Lowry, an old man riding hell for leather on the vengeance trail. Before he slid down from the rock he saw them reining in their horses. The place they stopped was well beyond the range of his Winchester.

"They're out there but they're coming in slow," he told Manning. "The old man isn't taking a chance on being ambushed. He's got three men with him. Let's get moving before he decides it's safe to come through here."

"How will he know that?"

"By pushing the others ahead and hanging back himself. That will take a while. Now we know what we're up against, so we can start to make some kind of plan."

They rode fast, putting distance behind them. By now they were far into the mountains, bare and brown, country as rugged as Sundance had seen in a hard-paced lifetime. He checked their back trail again, but there was no sign of Lowry and the three riders with him. They moved on again, pushing their horses as fast as they could go. Early in the afternoon they stopped to water the horses and to let them graze on what forage they could find. There wasn't much and the lack of food was beginning to tell on the horses. Only Eagle had the stamina for this kind of country.

"Have you made a plan yet?" Manning asked.

"Not yet," Sundance answered.

Manning said, "I wish the hell you would. I'm getting sick of this."

"You'll get sicker before it's done. You wanted excitement in the Wild West. Now you're complaining about it."

"Oh, not really," Manning said. "It will be something to think about in years to come. You still think I don't have a long life ahead of me? Yes. Yes. I know you think you're going to kill me. But there's more to killing a man than talking about it."

"I won't say much when the time comes. Most of the talk is coming from you."

Manning laughed. "Then I won't say another word."

By nightfall they were still miles ahead of their pursuers. Before the light failed, Sundance checked their back trail again and said they would move on for another few hours. All day William Manning kept the pace Sundance had set for them, but now he looked very tired, rubbing his eyes as if he couldn't see too well.

"We have to keep riding," Sundance told him. "In the dark maybe we can dodge them for a while and then you can rest."

"Whatever you say," William Manning said, and his voice was as weary as the rest of him.

Four hours later they settled down for the rest of the night on a rock-strewn slope with a clear field of fire behind it. There was a moon and it washed everything in pale yellow light. They watered the horses, but they were restless from hunger. William Manning fell into a deep sleep as soon as he lay down. Before he slept he offered to stand a watch. Sundance said no.

The brothers were asleep when Alison Manning came over to where Sundance sat behind a rock with his rifle cradled in his arms. She looked worn out.

"You should rest," Sundance said. "You won't be any good if you don't rest. If you can't sleep, at least close your eyes. It's not sleep but it helps."

"I'm afraid," she said. "When I close my eyes I see things I don't want to see."

"What do you see?"

"Not the old man. I see my husband killing all of us. I'm more afraid of him than I am of the old man. He likes you but he'll kill you too."

"He hasn't done it yet."

"But you can't be sure what he'll try. That's the way he is. All his life he's done as he's pleased, never thinking of anything or anybody. I ought to know. I've been married to him for seven years."

"Why did you marry him?" Sundance said quietly, wanting to take back the question as soon as he'd asked it. But he was going to kill her husband, he thought with grim humor. Why not ask the question?

Alison Manning made a strange sound. It might have been laughter. "I was young and didn't know what I wanted," she said. "And when I got it, I didn't want it. But it's hard to say no to Edward. I don't know if he really cared about me. I just knew it would be a blow to his pride to give me up. Now we've brought our troubles all the way to America. You may die because of us."

Sundance said, "No need to go on about that. I've been in trouble before."

"But I have to bring it up. Even if we escape, he'll try to kill us. You too."

Sundance looked over at Edward Manning asleep

159

under a blanket. Maybe he was asleep. "What are you suggesting, Mrs. Manning?"

"Kill him," she said with finality. "You'll die if you don't. You've killed men, but you aren't a killer. Edward is. He'll turn on you like the madman he is."

"You mean I should kill him while he sleeps?"

"Kill him any way you can."

"What does his brother think of this?" .

Alison Manning said, "William would never agree to it. He's not the strongest man in the world, but he's a good man. And he's better than my husband and I suppose he's better than me. Do it, Sundance. Do it now before it's too late."

"No deal," Sundance said. "I can't do it like that. I know you're right, but I can't do it like that. All I can do is be ready for him. Go back and get some sleep."

Alison Manning pulled away from him. "You're as mad as he is," she said.

Sundance said, "Everybody here is a little mad."

He settled down for the rest of his watch. The moon remained bright. There were no clouds in the sky. He wondered what the old man was doing out there in the darkness. At that moment he might be creeping close, a cartridge in the chamber of the Weatherby. The hours passed and he woke Manning for his turn of duty.

"Nothing?" Manning said when he stood up.

"Not so far," Sundance said. "That doesn't mean there won't be. If they come, don't fire back unless they're right on top of you. The old man may use the others to draw your fire."

"What time do we leave here?"

"If it looks good we'll try to whittle them down in the morning. We've been hiding and running. The old man may think we'll do that again."

"That's more like it," Manning said.

"I said we'll do it if it looks good," Sundance told him. "You say your wife can shoot. Your brother may not be up to much, the way he is, but we'll lay down plenty of lead. Try for the horses as much as the men. One's as good as the other."

"Just so long as we do something."

Sundance rolled himself in his blanket but didn't sleep. Through slitted eyes he saw Manning watching him. He lay for a while with his hand on his revolver, ready to blast Manning if he raised the rifle. The woman might be right; she knew her husband better than he did. Finally he knew there was nothing to be done other than killing the man. Manning was full of contradictions, peculiar shifts of character. He was an odd mixture of honor and treachery. Maybe he was afraid of being afraid. There were men like that, men who couldn't come to terms with their own nature. Throughout his life he had lived on the edge of danger, as if he courted death but was somehow afraid of it.

Sundance went to sleep at last, knowing that he might never wake up. He woke up to find Alison Manning watching him, a rifle in her hand. William Manning was awake too.

Alison Manning said, "Edward just crawled out there. His horse is still here. One moment he was here, the next he was gone."

It was about an hour before dawn. The light was thick and gray. "He's trying to get his rifle back," Sundance said.

Her eyes were hard. "Let him go," she said. "If they kill him it will give us a chance to get away. We'll be free of him for good."

Sundance told her to shut up. "The two of you get

over here and give me some cover. Hate him all you like, he's still on our side in this. Shoot him when we come in and I'll leave you. See how far you get."

They took up their positions and Sundance crawled out into the half light. Manning's tracks were in the sand and he followed them through a gap in the rocks. There was no way to tell how far he had gone. The tracks disappeared and picked up again on the other side of a flat rock. Then he saw Manning, still crawling, about fifty feet ahead, and just as he raised up to throw a pebble, a big man sprang from behind a rock with a knife in his hand. Manning turned as the knife came down and buried itself in the sand. The man threw himself on top of Manning. The knife came up again, this time aimed at his throat. By then Sundance was running silently in the sand. Manning had the attacker's knife hand in a grip, but it was inching down toward his throat. Sundance seized the attacker's neck with his forearm and turned it back until there was a soft snapping sound and the body went limp. Manning rolled the body away and took the knife from the dead man's hand.

"A big bastard, wasn't he?" Manning whispered.

"Get the hell away from here," Sundance said. "The ambush won't work now."

They were nearly back to the horses when the Weatherby boomed, but the light was too bad for any accurate shooting. Manning's wife and brother opened fire at the same time, firing as fast as they could jack the levers. The Weatherby fired again and the bullet whanged off a rock only inches from the woman's head.

"Run," Sundance yelled. "Don't shoot any more. He's firing at your flashes."

Bullets chased them out of camp. One of the spare

162

horses was hit and went down kicking and screaming. Away from camp, Sundance told them to walk the horses so the old man would think they were getting set up for a second ambush. Then, when they were too far away to be heard, they rode fast into the dawn.

"That's twice you've saved my life," Manning said to Sundance.

"Next time I won't try," Sundance said. "You were walking right into your own rifle."

"I must get that rifle. It would change everything."

Sundance shook his head. "When the time comes I'll take the rifle, not you."

Manning laughed. "Then that makes one more thing that has to be settled between us."

CHAPTER TWELVE

They found the water hole early that afternoon, a muddy puddle with animal tracks around it. Sundance and Manning stood guard while the others scooped out a hole in the mud. Slowly it began to fill with brackish water that had a bad taste and smell.

"It's all right," Sundance said after sipping at the first canteen to be filled. "If the animals drink it, it won't kill us. The old man must be as hard up for water as we are. This is where we'll kill him."

Manning drank some of the foul-tasting water. "How will we do that?"

Sundance said, "We have the water and he doesn't." He looked at William Manning, who was rubbing his eyes. "You lied when you said your head was all right. Back there you were shooting half blind."

"He was doing his best," Alison Manning said.

Sundance looked at William Manning again. "That's not the point. I have to know if he can shoot straight now."

"I'm afraid I can't shoot too well, Sundance."

"You never could," his brother said. "Even with a clear head you weren't that much of a shot. Perhaps you'd better give me your rifle."

"You keep the rifle," Sundance told William Manning. "Just don't waste ammunition firing at what you can't see. If they try to rush us, then you shoot. Understand?"

William Manning nodded. There were furrows of pain between his eyes. "I understand. You think they'll try to rush us?"

Sundance took a canteen from the water hole and stoppered it. "If they get thirsty enough they may do anything. A night attack is more likely than anything. Right now I'm going to set out a full canteen where they can see it."

"A devilish idea," Manning said.

"I want them to know we have water to spare," Sundance said. "The horses will go behind the rocks over there. They'll be safe enough if they aren't hit by ricochets. Now we wait and see what happens."

William Manning's position was close to the horses, while Sundance and the others spread out along the rim of the hollow. Manning's wife held her rifle so hard that her knuckles showed white. Sundance sighted in on the canteen standing on a rock about one hundred yards away. It would be an easy shot when the time came.

"I can see them," Manning said. "It's a pity these Winchesters don't have a better range."

Sundance didn't answer. Lowry and the two men had disappeared into a ravine a long way out. They would work their way under cover until they were close enough to shoot. The others had to get close, but the old man could sit back at more than five hundred yards. He could even stay back at six hundred and still kill with the scope.

Two Winchesters opened up from the end of the ravine, kicking up sand but doing no damage. Sundance waved the others to keep down, then he jerked the

Winchester and fired once. The Weatherby fired, but the old man hadn't been able to move the scope fast enough. Still, the bullet came close enough.

Sundance moved a few feet from where he was. The others did the same. The plan was to keep moving under cover so the old man wouldn't be able to do any accurate sighting.

"You want me to shoot the canteen?" Manning called out, grinning with excitement.

"Wait till the sun works on them for a while. They must have seen the canteen by now. Let them sweat."

The Winchesters started firing again, trying to provide a target for the Weatherby. There was a lull in the shooting, after which the bullets came from different positions, right and left of the water hole. When the Weatherby fired once more Sundance knew the old man was closer. His failure to score a hit must have angered him. Sundance could just about see him grinding his store teeth in an old man's fury.

An hour dragged by and then another. The sun beat down with relentless force. Manning looked at Sundance and he nodded back. Manning raised up and blew a hole in the canteen: a perfect, quick shot at one hundred yards. The instant he fired, the Weatherby boomed and the bullet tore the rifle from Manning's hands. The barrel was bent out of shape and he threw it away after jacking out the shells that remained in the magazine. Then he crawled over to his wife and took her rifle.

"Give her your belt gun," Sundance ordered. "You showed too much of yourself just now."

"I thought it was a fine shot," Manning said.

The firing went on as the sun slid down the sky, a ball of copper flame that would soon be gone. As soon as it got cooler, thirst wouldn't bother the old man so much. They were bound to try something during the night, but Sundance thought they could be held off. Darkness would take away Lowry's advantage, and the two men with him weren't so brave. Desperation wouldn't start to set in until the sun came up in the morning.

"What's the matter with your hand?" Sundance asked Manning.

"Got a bit banged up when the bullet hit my rifle. It's swollen, but I can use it. Pity it's my right hand. I'll know how good it is the next time I shoot."

Manning might be out of the fight if his hand got worse. There was no use telling him to crawl down and soak it in the water hole. The water was too warm and would stay that way for hours.

"Do we stay where are are after it gets dark?" Manning asked.

Sundance said no. "We'll move back and try to get them outlined here on the rim. We should be able to drive them off or kill them. I hope to hell you can shoot."

"I'll hold up my end. Hand or no hand, I'm a better shot than you are." Manning flexed his swollen fingers. "That, too, is a statement of fact. I hope you don't mind."

"It's time to move back," Sundance said. "Tell your brother to watch the back, though it's probably too hard to get over all those rocks."

They waited in darkness on the far side of the water hole. The wind blew across the top of the hollow, making a keening sound. Manning's wife looked dispirited and very tired, as if she didn't care anymore. She didn't utter a word, not even a whisper.

The attack came suddenly. Two men came over the

rim of the hollow, firing their rifles while the Weatherby boomed from the side. Sundance aimed and killed a man. Manning fired at the other and missed, cursing his hand as he did. Then the second man was gone, diving back the way he had come. Sundance ran to the top and fired at the second man as he darted into the rocks. The bullet blew the hat off his head, but he was in cover before Sundance could fire again. The Weatherby opened up from a distance, from high up, forcing Sundance to take cover. The firing stopped and Sundance rolled over the rim and began to crawl toward the old man's position. When he got there all he found were spent shell casings. He moved back to the water hole.

The dead man lay on his face, his rifle under him. Sundance took his rifle, ammunition, and belt gun. He handed the rifle to Alison Manning, who hadn't fired her revolver during the attack.

Sundance pointed to her holstered revolver. "You'll have to do better than that. The bullet you didn't fire could have killed one of us."

"She did as well as I did," Manning said angrily. "My damned hand failed me. It was such an easy shot."

"Get back to the rim," Sundance ordered. "Lowry hasn't given up yet. Sleep if you can. I'll watch for the old man."

Manning said, "I could have killed the other man, but I missed an easy shot."

Sundance whirled on him. "Stop whining about it and get back to the rim. There's only two of them now, so it isn't so bad. If we can kill the other man, Lowry will be alone."

The morning sun blazed up hot and fierce, without

even a puff of wind. During the night the water hole had filled up again and they drank from it without touching the canteens. Sundance dragged the body away and put it behind a rock. In that sun they would be smelling it if they stayed another day.

Looking at his damaged hand, Manning was in a sullen mood very different from his usual cockiness. He made a fist of it, gritting his teeth against the pain.

"Some of those fingers look broken," Sundance said, thinking it made no difference. Manning was finished as a hunter of animals—and men. As soon as he finished with Lowry, he would send Manning's wife and brother across to New Mexico. They had plenty of water now, they would make it all right. There were ranches in the foothills on the other side. They wouldn't starve if they cooked some horsemeat and took it along.

And he would stay with Manning and they would have it out.

Everything was sun and silence as the day wore on. There had been no shooting, not a single shot. Their rifle barrels were blistering hot to the touch and there was no shade anywhere except where the horses were. A gritty wind blew up for a while without bringing any relief. Furnace hot, it stung their eyes and drifted fine sand into the muddy water of the hole.

"What the hell is he doing out there?" Manning said. No one had spoken for an hour. The swelling in Manning's hand had gotten worse. Even the wrist was puffing up. "We ought to go after him and finish this."

"No," Sundance said. "Not having water will wear him down."

Manning had been sipping water. Now he spat it out. "You call this slop water?"

"Don't drink it if you don't want it," Sundance said.

170

"Do what you like about the water. We're not going after Lowry."

In sudden anger Manning placed his left hand on his gun. Sundance, knowing he could kill him at will, just looked at him. Manning said, "You've been looking at my bad hand and deciding I'm done for. That's what you've been thinking, isn't it?"

A shot rang out. It wasn't the Weatherby and the bullet didn't come anywhere near the water hole. "Go easy," Sundance yelled at Manning when he started to scramble up to the rim. He grabbed Manning's legs and brought him down, but he still managed to raise his head. "It's the other bandit and he's waving a flag of truce."

"Keep down, damn you," Sundance said. But he raised his own head by inches and when he did he saw that Manning was right. The last member of the Lowry gang was about two hundred yards away and waving a rifle with a strip of cloth tied to the muzzle. Still staying low, Sundance waved his hat and the man started forward at a hesitant walk.

"The old man wants to make a deal," Manning said.

"Like hell he does," Sundance said. "All he wants to do is kill."

"What's the harm in listening?"

"We'll listen, but it won't be on the square."

The man with the flag of truce was getting closer. "What do you want? Come ahead if you want to talk."

The man had stopped. "I can't see you," he called back.

"You're not supposed to. I asked you what you want. Stop where you are and say what you want." Sundance couldn't see the man. He figured he was less than a hundred yards away.

171

The man yelled back, "Lowry wants to make a trade. Give us water and we'll pull out. That's the truth. We're bone dry. It's not worth it, Lowry says. Lowry gives you his word of honor he'll pull out. What do you say?"

For an answer, Sundance shot the man in the chest. He was still falling when the Weatherby fired. Sundance felt the hot wind of the bullet in his face, but he wasn't hit. Other bullets came and then they stopped.

Lying on his back, Sundance levered a cartridge. "There's your deal. Lowry's out of water and out of time. I think Lowry held the rifle on his own man and made him walk up here. He's like that."

"You still haven't got my rifle."

"I'll get it."

"Then you intend to kill me?"

Sundance had been thinking about Manning's hand. It went against the grain to gun down a crippled man, yet he knew he was thinking like Manning—the schoolboy code. He had come too far to let this so-called code stand in the way of justice. Because that's what it was. Stripped of fancy words and pious sentiments, there was no other name for it.

"How well can you shoot a pistol with your left hand?" he asked the Englishman.

Manning's eyes narrowed. "Nearly as well as with the right. I just can't fire a rifle left-handed. How good are you with the left?"

"Fair," Sundance said. "I had to learn one time. If you want to do it like I say, we can pace off, one pistol bullet apiece, and that will be the end of it. If you kill me you'll be free to go."

Manning's voice held a note of incredulity. "A duel! You're talking about a duel. Where do you think you are? Paris, sixty years ago?"

172

Sundance said, "It's your choice, Manning. It's as fair as I can make it."

"Why are you giving me this chance?"

"I don't know, Manning. We've been through all this together. Maybe that's part of the reason. Don't think it's because I like the way you think. You want to go ahead with it, after Lowry is dead? Nothing can be settled till the old man is dead."

"Why not?" Manning said. "I've never been in a duel. They hang you in England for dueling." His voice became mocking. "Will there be seconds and all that sort of thing? My dear wife and brother—"

"I don't want them here," Sundance said. "They'll get all the water they need to get to New Mexico. After that they'll have to shift for themselves."

"This whole thing is faintly ridiculous," Manning said. "A duel in the year 1887. But if that's the way you want it, I have no objection. I knew you were a special sort of fellow when I hired you. I regret that you haven't been paid the second thousand dollars."

"Your rifle is worth most of that," Sundance said. "The old man has the money he took from your wallet. I'll be paid. I always get paid for what I do. You'll back me when I go after Lowry?"

"Of course, old man. What are friends for? When do you want to do it?"

"When he settles in for the night."

"Then you think he hasn't pulled out?"

"No," Sundance said. "His men are dead or have deserted him. He has some of your money, but he won't see that as enough. Hate will keep him here because that's all he has left. He'll stay on till the end.

"We can't start your wife and brother till the old man is dead. If he circles our camp he could be waiting for

173

them on the trail."

Manning nodded. "I agree. I'd hate to see anything happen to my dear wife, not to mention my wonderful brother."

"They're not such bad people."

"They're not such good people."

"If you live, let them go."

"That's a lot to ask, Sundance. After all I am the lady's legal husband."

"That's bullshit and you know it."

"That's true, but I like the sound of it. Of course this conversation may be meaningless not too many hours from now."

"Maybe so," Sundance agreed. "Let's figure out how we're going to kill the old man. He'll be in a place where we can't get at his back, so we'll have to go at him straight on. He'll fire and then have to load another cartridge. How long does that take you?"

"About three seconds," Manning said, making an ejecting and reloading motion with his swollen right hand. "I've done it in less, but he isn't as fast as I am. But I've heard him shoot and he's fast enough. That was in daylight though. At night he may be slower. He fires at me and you rush him, is that it?"

Sundance said, "I can't think of any other way to do it. If you can, then tell me."

"It's good enough," Manning said.

Sundance was glad it was close to being over. He cleaned the Winchester, blowing grit from the barrel. Then he unloaded and reloaded before he wrapped it in a blanket until they were ready to take on Lowry. Manning sat below the rim watching his wife and brother. A strange group of people, Sundance thought. Obviously, the things that tormented Manning had driven him over the edge in some ways. His brother looked like a dreamer and he was a drunk. Alison Manning, what was she? He just didn't know.

Before too long it was time to go. The sky was darkening and there were things to be done. Manning looked at Sundance and nodded.

"Keep a close watch," Sundance told Manning's wife. "We're going to look for the old man. If we find him you'll be all right. We can't have him behind us. You understand?"

She made an odd gesture with her hand that he had come to know. "You've been good to us," she said. "Whatever happens, I won't forget you."

"Sure," Sundance said.

The sky grew darker, with hardly a glimmer of light when they crawled over the rim and started the other way. It was quiet except for some small, twittering creature, and though the sun was gone, the sand was warm. Over the rim, they separated and went to the right and left. Sundance knew it might take hours to find Lowry. He might not even be close. The old man knew all the outlaw tricks and would use them now. His dirty world had come apart, yet he would try to go on living out of sheer viciousness.

Sundance lay in the sand and listened. The night creature had scampered away and nothing broke the silence. He crawled on holding the Winchester across his arms, careful not to let it get fouled by sand. When he had gone far enough from the water hole he stood up, waiting for gunfire to erupt from the darkness. It remained quiet as he went ahead, listening for sounds.

He stopped again when he was about a quarter of a mile from the water hole. Here and there he searched in rocky places that the old man might hole up in. Always he was aware that the next search might be his last, for Lowry wasn't just any old owlhooter, but a cunning killer who had survived for nearly sixty years by being smarter than the trash he ran with. Manning was somewhere to the left of him, though he couldn't tell how close. He advanced again, the Winchester cocked and ready, knowing that it all might be a waste of time. The old man could be near or far. He could be anywhere.

Now he was deep in a rocky defile with absolutely no light. Unable to see, he moved one silent step at a time. Reaching out to touch the walls of the defile he found a narrow ledge that slanted upward. He started to climb it, not knowing that it might drop off in a broken place. But it continued on that same long slant, then it widened and went in under the overhanging rock. Even before he heard the old man's breathing, he knew this was it. It was hardly a cave at all, just a place scooped out of the rock. Inside, he heard and smelled the old man. Lowry was asleep, his sixty-year-old body exhausted. This time Lowry had driven himself too hard. Death was going to be his punishment. Sundance edged toward him.

Lowry woke with a snarl when Sundance's foot touched an empty can, shifting it slightly. Not wanting to risk damaging the Weatherby, Sundance dropped his rifle and sprang forward with his knife. It clanged against rock as Lowry rolled away. Sundance leaped again and the old man's hands came up to block the downward thrust. He roared as the knife blade sank into his hand. There was the quick spatter of blood. Lowry was roaring like a maddened beast, fighting to the last. Sundance drove the knife into his side and the old man roared again. He tried to bring his knee up into Sundance's crotch. The knife was stuck in his ribs and Sundance had to turn it to get it out. There was blood

176

on the haft as well as the blade. Sundance, sickened by the old man's smell, drove the blade up under the ribcage with all the strength he could muster. Lowry's body jerked once and the life went out of it.

Sundance struck a match. It flared bright in the darkness. Lowry lay on his side, his artificial teeth bared in a snarl. Sundance wiped the blade and put it in his belt. The Weatherby stood against the rock wall and the old man's dirty denim coat had cartridges in all the pockets. The match went out, but Sundance didn't need to strike another one. There was no food. The canteen was empty.

He was starting down the ledge when a six-shooter roared and bullets smacked into rock. More bullets came and swung back under the shelter of the rock. He bolted a round and yelled, "I'm coming after you, Manning. You went back on your word, you son of a bitch."

Manning shouted, "Try to catch me, Sundance." Then Sundance heard him running, but didn't fire at what he couldn't see. He had the rifle now, and he would use it on its owner. Manning had turned on him again, for the last time, he vowed.

He got down and started back. Manning had a small start on him, but he'd catch him just the same. Somehow, the Englishman's nerve had failed him at the end. All the talk about living and dying poker-faced was a sham. He knew Sundance would kill him if they faced off with pistols. Or if he wasn't sure, he was afraid to go through with it. It was like he'd said so many long days before: the big game he should never had given a chance.

Sundance walked holding the rifle, still wary, but moving fast. He reached the end of the defile when he

177

heard two shots placed close together. Then he heard four more. Manning was killing his wife and brother. It couldn't be anything else. Sundance felt a sudden tightness in his head, as he thought of the bodies he would find. No need to hurry now.

Manning might be waiting for him below the rim of the water hole. He moved in with a bolted round in the chamber. Then he heard hoofs beating on the ground. Manning was gone. Sundance put his ear to the ground and the sound of the hoofs grew fainter, then disappeared altogether.

Sundance heard a whinny in the darkness and Eagle came toward him. The stallion was lathered with sweat and there was a bullet crease in his neck. Sundance didn't touch the wound. All he said was, "Follow along, boy."

Manning's wife and brother lay dead by the water hole. He gathered brush from the rocks and started a fire. Manning wasn't coming back, or Eagle would have whinnied a warning. When the fire blazed up, Sundance looked at the bodies. They had been shot in the head. The horses had been killed by bullets. Eagle had broken out before Manning could shoot again.

In his haste, Manning had left three canteens behind in the dark. Now Sundance drank from one of them and refilled it to the top. He called Eagle close and told the horse to hold still. The bullet crease hadn't drawn much blood. It would heal in a few days.

"Drink your fill, boy," Sundance said, pointing to the water hole."

He heaped more wood on the fire, and while it was burning down to cooking coals, he covered the bodies with rocks to keep them from the coyotes and buzzards. It wasn't much of a funeral for a woman like Alison

Manning. No Christian, he said no prayers.

He cooked a steak he cut from the youngest of the horses, the first food he'd eaten for days. The fire burned down by the time he was ready to go. He thought of the wild old man now stiffening in the rocky defile. He thought of the men he had killed, men whose names he never learned. And he thought of Alison Manning and the night they had talked by the fire.

It was time for a reckoning.

CHAPTER THIRTEEN

Manning had a Winchester and a fair amount of ammunition. He had a horse and plenty of water. And he had about two hours start. Those were the cold facts.

Sundance pushed on for the rest of the night, always watching for an ambush. Whatever else he was, Manning was a resourceful man, as Sundance was himself. And knowing that there could be no mercy now, he would use every ruse he'd learned in his years as a soldier and a hunter. Yet the hunted man always was at a disadvantage, if for no other reason than he was running for his life. Some hunted men wanted to be killed because of the enormity of their crime. There would be none of that with Manning. His crime wouldn't bother him, and that put him slightly ahead.

Sundance considered all this as he rode toward the dawn. The more you knew about a man, the easier it was to kill him. Yet there was something about Manning's character that eluded him. He might never find out what it was.

When dawn flooded the mountains with light, he was able to pick up Manning's trail. Two bald mountains were close together, and he followed the trail between them. He followed the trail through a long, rocky valley with dry grass growing up its sides. Here, Manning had allowed his horse to graze. Hoofprints were in the grass, and then they went on.

Sundance dismounted and looked down the valley through the scope. It was dry and empty, with nothing moving except the wind-blown grass. He moved the scope here and there, into a pile of rocks, into a place where the grass grew tall. Satisfied that Manning wasn't there, he rode on till he reached the southern end of the valley. There it narrowed and finally petered out. Then he had to climb again, this time along the side of another mountain, and Manning's trail was ahead of him all the time.

Sundance could see that Manning wasn't pushing his horse too hard, the worst mistake a hunted man can make. He found an empty canteen and knew that Manning had stopped there to water his horse. They were in New Mexico now, Sundance figured, but there was no way to be sure. There was a long stretch where he had to lead the stallion, picking his way across broken rock. He came to a place where the trail led across a rockfall, and then there was another dry valley that went on for miles. The mountains rose up on both sides. In the valley itself, traveling was easy. Disregarding the danger, Sundance took his horse to the other end at a gallop. Manning was making better time than he expected. If Manning got all the way to the far side of the mountains, there was a chance he could lose himself in the trails that ran through the foothills. There was a railroad stop not far from Santa Fe, a place called Lamy. Trains that stopped there connected with trains that went all the way to New York, Philadelphia, New Orleans, all the big cities on the East Coast. The Southern Pacific went clear to El Paso. That was as good as being in Mexico.

In the late afternoon, Sundance found a wet patch of ground in the shadow of a rock. Manning had been there not long before, or else the ground would be dry by now. The horse had slopped the water in Manning's hat. It was the first real sign that he was close. Maybe just thirty minutes ahead. Or just a few hundred yards. Waiting with the Winchester behind a rock.

Sundance dismounted and told Eagle to stay where he was. A man on a horse made too good a target. He was getting used to the feel of the Weatherby. No wonder Manning thought so highly of it. It was heavy, but the balance was perfect, the action smooth. Yet it felt strange to carry a rifle that had hunted him in the hands of another man, and he wondered if the beautiful rifle had been the real inspiration for the manhunt. The wife and brother might have been afterthoughts. The murders might have been committed out of hatred of himself, the knowledge that he was much less a man than he thought he was and always had believed himself to be. The man killed, not the rifle. On the other hand, possession of the rifle might have put thoughts of murder into Edward Manning's head.

Sundance sighted through the scope and picked up nothing but a ground nesting bird hopping in the grass. Manning wasn't there, or the bird would be gone. The scope picked up other birds, then a marmot skittering from rock to rock. Manning wasn't there.

Darkness came and there was no moon. Sundance dismounted and walked beside his horse. His own feet made no sounds, but Eagle's hoofs could be heard no matter how slowly they moved. Once again Manning had the advantage, and it was going to be like that until the deadly game ended with one of them dead. There were more mountains ahead, the last high country before the flatland. He could see the peaks jagged against the dull dark-blue of the night sky. This last stretch was going to be tougher than what had gone on before, and maybe there was no way through to the other side. A man could cross just about any mountain if he had plenty of food and water, ropes and climbing equipment—and if he had enough time to do it.

Sundance moved on in darkness, waiting for the moon to show itself. He would be in danger the moment it did. Most men couldn't shoot well by moonlight, but Manning wasn't like most men. There might be a pass through the mountains, or a series of long gaps. A man would have to move from one to the other. All that would take hard climbing in places no horse could go. Sundance guessed he would have to leave Eagle again, but there was no helping that. If Manning got away he'd be convinced that nothing could stop him, and even if he found a safe place he wouldn't stay there. Sooner or later the devil in his brain would send him out again, and Sundance wasn't even sure that Manning wouldn't try to stalk him again in some place far from where they were now.

It got colder and he knew from the force of the wind that the mountains were even higher than he'd figured. There might be snow up there even at this time of the year. He gave water to the stallion and drank a little himself. The peaks looked closer now, even in the half-darkness, and then the moon came out and he could see the menacing upthrust of rock that lay ahead. He stopped moving when the moon broke through the clouds. Now there were shadows instead of solid darkness. Any shadow was a place of concealment, a place to shoot from.

He unsaddled Eagle and told the stallion to stay behind before he went on, staying in the shadows as best he could. Stooping in a patch of moonlight he looked for hoofprints and found them. The tracks went on. Here, there were no foothills. The rock wall of the mountains rose up abruptly. In the moonlight the peaks looked like the gothic spires of cathedrals or fanciful castles in children's books. A mile from where he started he found Manning's horse. The son of a bitch hadn't taken the time to unsaddle the animal.

Suddenly he knew what Manning was going to do: climb by night and try to hole up by day. If he could do that, the scope on the Weatherby wouldn't mean much. So there was nothing to do but follow Manning in the dark, climb up to places that were dangerous even by day. He smiled. Manning was daring him to do it. Risk his life for revenge as old Lowry had done, and, in doing so, lose it. Maybe Manning pictured him as seething with bloodlust, so eager to kill that he would take chances he didn't have to. It would be good if Manning thought that. Anything Manning was wrong about would bring him closer to losing the deadliest game of all.

With the rope coiled over his shoulder, Sundance began the long climb. At first it was easy. There was a wide split in the rock and he went up into it without having to look for footholds. There was a place where he had to heave himself onto a narrow shelf, and then the fissure began again. He couldn't tell if Manning had gone this way; a boot left no marks on the rock. There was nothing to do but keep on climbing until daylight. Then the waiting would begin. Coming from below, he would make a better target than Manning. The shooter on the high ground always held better cards.

He rested, sweating in the cold. Now the peaks had disappeared and all he could see was the rock in front of his face. The rock gave way to a patch of brush, and when he found some of it broken and flattened he knew he wasn't climbing after nothing. Clouds sailed across the moon, shutting out the watery light. He stayed where he was, waiting for the light to come again. But it didn't, and now it was darker than before.

He hitched the rope to keep it from slipping and started climbing again. Getting through the tangled brush, the canteen came loose from his belt and he had to stop to tie it again. In a while he came to a place where the rock leveled out and there were stunted trees and more brush. The step in the side of the mountain ran back for about two hundred yards before the rock started again. At first, hampered by darkness, he could find no break in it, and it took him about ten minutes of groping to find one. This was narrower than the others, and once in it he couldn't even see his hands as they reached up for a hold that would take him higher.

Halfway up he stopped when he heard a sound. Flattening himself against the rock, he listened again. From the darkness above came three shots spaced close together. Flame jetted and lead spattered on the rock close to his head. A sliver of rock cut his forehead and brought a ribbon of blood that ran into his eye. Still he didn't move because there wasn't enough room to maneuver the Weatherby.

"Are you down there, old man?" Manning's voice called from above. "You're not going to get me, you know. Why don't you say something? After all, we've been through so much together. Come on up then if you won't speak. I may be waiting for you. Think about this. Is it worth it?"

Sundance stayed where he was, waiting for more bullets to come. Manning knew he wasn't dead because there had been no sound of a falling body. He moved up. If he didn't, daylight would catch him there. The Weatherby scraped against the rock and he braced himself for bullets. Nothing happened and he knew Manning was gone, still climbing, making the most of the last hour of darkness.

First light was gray on the side of the mountain. The wind blew hard, stirring patches of brush. At first the mountain was gray-brown and then it was red, which made it even more forbidding. The red faded as the light grew stronger.

He lay in a patch of brush and used the scope to see what was up above. Nothing. It was just the way he'd figured. A long day of waiting. The other man's mockery meant nothing to him. It didn't change his feelings one way or another, and maybe it was a good sign. Once a man began to run off at the mouth, usually it was an indication that he wasn't so sure of himself. But he decided not to decide about Manning's state of mind at this point. Manning could insult the memory of his mother, and all he would do was keep coming with the same unfeeling resolution. He had good cover and some water, and that was all he needed at the moment. From where he was, he had a good view of a long flat rock that sloped up from a scatter of rocks. It was easy enough to climb. He guessed Manning was somewhere at the top of it. There would have been enough time to get there after the shooting and the brave words.

He knew the waiting wouldn't bother Manning as it would other men. Waiting was a part of a hunter's life and as important as courage and marksmanship. Sundance figured they were about equally matched in that respect. The sun grew warm but the wind still blew. Sundance closed his eyes and slept, though not fully asleep, not fully awake. If any sound came he would be ready to spring into action without even an instant's confusion. It was something he had trained himself to do. More than once, it had saved his life.

He lay like that for three hours. When he opened his eyes nothing had changed except that the sun was higher in the sky and the barrel of the Weatherby was hot to the touch. Two swallows of water were all he allowed himself before he stoppered the canteen and prepared himself to wait until darkness came again.

It came with the shadows, with the sudden chill in the wind, as the sun went behind the peaks, making its descent toward the far horizon. It looked like Manning was heading straight up into the peaks instead of trying to find some way around them. It couldn't be that he wasn't aware of the danger in that. There would come a time when he could climb no higher. Was he trying to place himself in a position from which there could be no retreat? A place where his courage, or lack of it, would be established once and for all? And if he died a coward there no one ever to know?

Just so he dies, Sundance thought.

He moved on, climbing up the side of the rock. Before he got to the top, he lay still, hardly breathing. He gave it five minutes. By the end of the night they would be far up the mountain. During the night he found more broken brush, this time in places that Manning could have avoided without too much trouble. It looked like Manning was deliberately leaving the only trail he could.

The next day passed like the one before. Sundance slept and sipped water when he felt the need. The wind blew and the sun set. That was all.

That night the climbing was worse, with fewer steps in the rock. Even the brush had given out. They were at the

188

summit of the mountain and only the last peak remained, an almost smooth pillar of rock that rose for hundreds of feet. Sundance no longer had any doubt that Manning intended to make his stand there. There could be no other reason for the climb. Having decided that, Sundance felt even calmer than before. Yet along with the feeling of peace there was a profound weariness. The whole terrible thing never should have happened. In spite of himself he felt a sort of pity for Manning. He had come so far to die for nothing.

Just so he dies, Sundance thought.

Sometime in the night he thought he heard Manning moving above him, but he made no attempt to use his handgun. On the sheer rock it would have been madness to try to use the Weatherby. Anyway, there was no hurry, and he waited until the sound faded.

He knew he had to find a place to shoot from by the time morning came. There was a ridge in the rock, just enough to give him a foothold. He made his way along it, holding on with his hands as best he could. There was gray in the sky by the time the ridge broadened into a ledge where he could stand without having to hold on. He looked up and he could see the sky. This was it, this would have to do.

There was a shell in the chamber of the Weatherby and it was ready to fire the instant Manning showed his head. He uncoiled the rope from his shoulder and placed it far behind him on the ledge. Going back down —if he didn't go off the ledge with bullets in him— there were places where the rope would be needed.

As the sky turned gray, he looked up at the top of the peak. Suddenly Manning's voice called out. It sounded thin in the great emptiness that surrounded them. There was no echo, nothing for the sound to roll against.

"Answer me, Sundance," Manning called. "Where are you, old man?"

"Shoot and find out," Sundance shouted back. "I'm down here."

"Where is that, old fellow?"

"What are you waiting for, Manning?" Sundance yelled. "You want your rifle back, climb down and get it."

There was a burst of wild laughter from the top. "I can always get another Weatherby. But for now, don't let anything happen to the one you have."

This was no place to use the scope. The range was too short. He held it chest-high, ready to swing it to his shoulder when Manning fired the first shot. It came right after Manning's last word, but he fired so fast and ducked back so fast that there was no time to get a shot at him. The bullet didn't come close.

"Your aim is off," Sundance yelled.

"I wasn't aiming." Manning was laughing again. "You didn't even fire."

Sundance wasn't sure how long Manning would keep this up. If he wanted to be theatrical, he had come to the right place for it. The sun blazed down on endless miles of mountains and there wasn't a cloud in the sky.

"You're not much for conversation, are you, Sundance?" Manning shouted. "It's not that we don't have a lot to talk about. I know. I know. You never discuss politics or religion. Then what about women? You liked my wife, didn't you? Can't blame you, old man."

This time Sundance nearly blew Manning's head off when he fired at him. There was silence after that. The sun grew hotter and there were buzzards soaring overhead, attracted by the gunfire.

They've come for us, one of us, Sundance thought.

As the sun moved across the sky it would be harder on Manning than it was on him. Up where he was there would be no shadows, just baking rock.

Manning was shouting again. "I still have water, Sundance. What would you give for a drink of water? Climb on up and we'll have a drink of water, pretend it's something stronger, and talk about old times at the top of the world. You don't want to? The trouble with you, old man, you take a narrow view of things. You wouldn't be clinging to the side of a mountain if you didn't. You see everything in terms of right and wrong. There's no such thing. Or to put it another way, right is when you get what you want, wrong is when you don't."

Sundance knew from the sound of Manning's voice that he had moved to another position. He moved back along the ledge, feeling for the coiled rope with his heel. If he looked behind him for an instant, it might mean his death. With his back to the rock, he looked up, waiting for a shot at Manning's head. But no chance came, and the buzzards hadn't gone away.

Sundance wondered how much water Manning had left. His own was gone because he'd given most of it to his horse. If the son of a bitch had enough water, he would stay up there for at least another day, maybe more than that. And if Manning changed his mind about dying gloriously, he might use his rope to try to make a descent from the other side.

Manning shouted, "How is it down there, Sundance? The way things are going, we'll be here for a week. Admit it, there's no way you can get at me. You can't climb up without getting killed, and I'm not going to come down."

Sundance decided to keep him talking. Talking was

191

thirsty work even for a man accustomed to the tropics.

"Manning, you don't have to die up there. I can't let you go, but you'll have to stand trial. With your money you'll get off with no more than twenty years. That's better than dying on a chunk of rock."

No bullets came. Manning was laughing. "Is that your best offer, old man? Well, I have a better offer for you. Throw your guns out far so I can see them fall, then I'll give you safe passage to the bottom. Just go away from here. Go back to your Indians. It will be hard to say goodbye, but we'll always have our memories, won't we?"

"No deal, Manning," Sundance shouted. "I guess I'll have to come after you."

"Do that, old man. But there's only one way up and that's the way I came. I've checked. I think my offer is better than your offer. Come up the way I came and you'll get killed. If I kill you I'm going to see that this peak is named after you. Let's call it a mount instead of a peak. Mount Sundance."

The sun was well past the midpoint of the day, and hearing no shots, the buzzards were wheeling in closer.

"I'm still coming up," Sundance shouted. "But not just yet."

Manning laughed. "In the dark, naturally. I don't know about that, old man. I'd say that's a bit risky. But if you insist, who am I to stop you? The sun will be gone soon, then you'll have your chance. I must say it's been nice knowing you."

Sundance couldn't see the sun now. There had to be another way up. No matter how dangerous it was, he had to find another way to the top. As soon as it got dark he would try to find it.

Night came fast as it does in hot places. Manning was

silent now. Sundance made his way along the ledge, feeling the rock with his hands. In darkness, he reached out and found nothing that would give him a hold, then he reached out farther and higher. His fingers found a crack. He was standing at the end of the ledge. Four feet away, on the other side, it began again, but was no more than a few inches wide. That was enough to get his toes in if he had something to hold onto with his fingers. There was nothing to do but risk trying to get across by gripping the crack above his head and letting his feet swing free. If the crack ran around the side of the rock, there was a chance that he would find a place where he could climb higher. If he didn't find it, then he wouldn't get Manning.

He reached up high, dug his fingers into the crack and stepped sideways off the ledge, kicking out with his right leg. The sudden weight of his body, held only by his fingers, almost tore his arms from their sockets. Then his right leg touched the ledge. For a moment, unable to move, he hung there above the yawning darkness. He moved his left foot and got a better grip, then he moved his fingers through the crack until he was able to bring his left leg across. Now with both toes on the ledge he was able to relax some of the pressure on his arms. There wasn't a sound at the top.

After his shoulder sockets stopped hurting, he moved his fingers again. The crack in the rock seemed to go on. He edged along the ledge, reaching out with his right toe, then moving on. Every few minutes he was forced to stop and rest. It's going to take hours, he thought.

The moon came and went and he was still on the ledge, still looking for a place where he could climb. In all that time Manning hadn't uttered a word. That could mean he knew where he was. If so, all his efforts would end in death and he would go plummeting into darkness like a stone.

He rested again. His lungs were on fire and his fingers had no feeling. Then he found it, a hole in the rock, and then another. Before he started to climb he tried to work his fingers by freeing one hand, then the other. There was nothing he could do about the numbness in his feet. He started to go up.

He didn't know what time it was. It could be the middle of the night, it could be an hour till morning. He had to go up on a slant because the holes weren't positioned one above the other. It was too dark to see how far he had come. The wind gusted up and he couldn't move on until it died. Once again he began to climb.

His whole body stiffened when his fingers touched the top of the rock. But maybe it wasn't the top, just another ledge. He held on with one hand and reached in with the other. He stepped up into another hole and reached his hand all the way in. He was at the top.

He heaved his body over the edge and lay still, trying to control his tortured breathing. Somewhere in the darkness he heard Manning as he shifted his position. There was no other sound. Quivering with pain and fatigue, he unlimbered the Weatherby and went forward one step at a time.

There was a yell and Manning's rifle flamed in the dark. Sundance fired at the flash and Manning went down. There was no need to bolt another round. Manning was dead.

Sundance waited for dawn.

Morning came and the sun was a bloody ball of fire. Sundance looked down at Manning's body. The ruddy face was relaxed, almost smiling, as if he had found at last what he had searched for all his life—death. Now that he was dead, and there would be no more victims to his madness, Sundance found he could not muster any hatred for the man. Hating the dead was as futile as regretting the past.

Manning would stay there until the buzzards found him. And when his flesh was gone, his clothes and his bones would blow away. Nothing would remain.

Sundance, after one last look, started down the mountain to look for his horse. He wanted to forget the Mannings and everything that had brought them to this corner of the world, but that wasn't possible, not only because of the law, but because of himself. He felt he had to explain what had happened. If he did that, then he wouldn't have to think about it any more.

But the law had to be told, and that had nothing to do with his own feelings. It wouldn't be an easy story to tell; it might even be harder to find a lawman who would believe it. It all started in Trinidad, and that was where he would go, back all the way he had come, past the water hole where the man and the woman lay buried. He thought of the night beside the campfire with the woman. It was strange to think of her dead.

They're all dead, he thought.

All but me.

Coming down from the peaks he thought about how he would tell his story to the law. Finally, he gave up and decided to tell it just the way it happened. Maybe he was making a mistake in going to the law, but what else was there to do?

Eagle was waiting. "I'm sorry, boy," Sundance said, patting the great stallion's neck. "I got you into this."

Sundance mounted up for the long ride.

CHAPTER FOURTEEN

The marshal of Trinidad, J.T. Sowerby, was a small, quick-eyed man in early middle age. He sat back tugging his beard while Sundance told his story. The whole thing sounded crazy, but the marshal didn't even raise his tufted eyebrows. He had the look of a clever man with his town under control who was doing all right for himself. To Sundance he had the look of a careful crook, a humorous one, a soft-voiced crook who wouldn't go too far and therefore ruin what he had. He was very good at his job, Sundance knew.

"You're taking a chance coming back with a story like that," he said. "Another man might think you made the whole thing up."

"There's Edward Manning's wallet on your desk," Sundance said. "He killed his wife and brother. I can tell you where to find the bodies."

"I don't get to leave town much," Sowerby said. "Now what about Lowry Jenner? I might be interested in that. There's a lot of reward money riding on that old boy. You mean to say you don't want to claim any of it?"

"I'm no bounty hunter," Sundance said. "But you're a lawman. That's different. I can tell you how to find Lowry."

Marshal Sowerby smiled. "Well, it would be nice for folks to know he's finally dead. A public service, is what I mean. Once folks know he's dead, they can rest easy, knowing his murdering days are over. Yes sir, I just might take a look down that way. You sure you don't want any of the poster money?"

"Not a cent."

"Well, that's just fine. You say you took Manning's money off Lowry's body."

"That's right."

"You wouldn't be holding anything back, would you? Not that I'd blame you a whole lot if you did. You understand, I have to ask these questions so I can clear up this mess. Give you a clean slate, so to speak."

Sundance said, "I was owed a thousand and I took it. You think I didn't earn it?"

"Lord no," the marshal said, combing his silky beard with his fingers. "But I got to look at this from every angle. That's the law business for you. Everything is red tape and questions. What I'm saying is, I have to be sure of my facts. You take anything else that belonged to Manning? When he was here at the hotel, there was talk of the fine English rifle he had. A man told me it was the finest rifle he ever saw in his life."

"I took the rifle," Sundance said.

"I don't see it," the marshal said. "I don't see it here in my office. The way I look at it, it should go back to Manning's next of kin. The rifle, the money here on my desk, that would kind of wrap things up. I'd hate to have to hold you here, you understand, but the county sheriff is a lot more suspicious than I am. That man asks no end of questions. Might even bring you to trial. All he'll know is that you started out with these rich foreigners and came back alone. There was a case not so

198

different from this some years back. The man—the guide—got hung."

"I'd still like to keep the rifle," Sundance said.

"Of course you would. So would I. But the law's the law and there's no getting around it. I'm going to have to ask you to hand it over, Mr. Sundance. You don't have it hid, do you?"

Sundance said no. "It's with my horse."

"That's dandy," the marshal said. "Why don't we go get it and come back here so you can make a statement and sign it? That way there'll be a record if the country sheriff comes snooping around."

Sundance didn't want to give up the rifle, not to the marshal, not to anyone. This was irrational, he knew, but he had done such things before. No man was a machine. Feelings were facts. He hadn't thought much about the big rifle until the marshal said he wanted it. He knew the rifle, or Manning's money, never would get to England.

"You heard what I said?" the marshal asked. "I just explained the facts to you."

Sundance said, "I'd like to buy Manning's rifle."

"That might be against the law, to sell what ain't mine. But supposing it was possible, how much is it worth to you? We're just supposing now."

"Manning told me he paid about seven hundred and fifty dollars," Sundance said.

Marshal Sowerby pulled his beard and said, "Make it a thousand. An even thousand and we'll call it a day. We'll call that expenses for looking around in the mountains, burying the bodies and so forth."

Sundance just wanted to get out of Trinidad. What the marshal said about the county sheriff might be true. County law was always quarreling with town law.

"Make it nine hundred and fifty," he said. "I've got to have eating money for a while. I can manage on fifty."

Marshal Sowerby opened a drawer and put Manning's wallet in it. "Far be it for me to take a man's last cent," he said. "Let's see the money."

Sundance counted out ten one hundred dollar bills. "You'll have to make change," he said.

Marshal Sowerby produced his own wallet and put a fifty on the desk. "There you go," he said. "Everything neat and legal. You got a clear conscience and so do I. Leave no loose ends, is what I always say. You won't be coming back to Trinidad, will you?"

"No," Sundance answered. "But what about the statement I'm supposed to sign?"

The marshal got up from his desk and opened the door. "I'll see about the statement. No need to worry about a thing. I'll make you as pure as the driven snow. Just don't come back to Trinidad. It wouldn't be wise."

Sundance rode out of town. A few people stared at him, as people did everywhere. A few miles out he dismounted and smashed the rifle against a rock. He kept on hitting the rock until the rifle was nothing but splintered wood and twisted metal. Then he threw it far from him, and found that all his cold anger was gone. In just a few weeks he had been to hell and back, and all he had to show for it was fifty dollars.

But he was all right again. He had his horse, a fifty dollar bill, and the sun was shining. A lot of work remained to be done.

"Let's go, boy," Sundance said. He climbed into the saddle and rode away.

MAVERICK SHOWDOWN
By W. F. Bragg

PRICE: $1.75   LB910
CATEGORY: Western

COME HELL OR HIGH WATER, HE'D TAKE
IN THE MURDERER KNOWN AS KING KOLL!
MAVERICK SHOWDOWN
A HARD-HITTING WESTERN BY
MASTER STORYTELLER
W. F. BRAGG

FIRST TIME IN PAPERBACK

MOUNTAIN SHOOTOUT!

Silver Jack Steele was tracking the notorious murderer known as King Koll. High in the mountains, Silver Jack began to close in. He was feeling pretty confident, until guns appeared from behind every rock and bullets flew!

A NEST OF RATTLERS
By Martin Ryerson

PRICE: $1.95 LB924
CATEGORY: Western

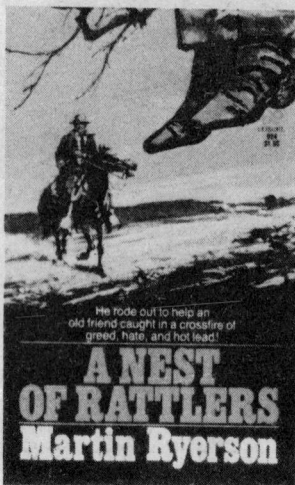

He rode out to help an old friend caught in a crossfire of greed, hate, and hot lead!

A NEST OF RATTLERS
Martin Ryerson

HOT LEAD CROSSFIRE!
Wes Thorne rode out to help his buddy Jim Randall, who was crippled by a bullet in his back, and losing control of his 5,000-head ranch. To regain control for Randall, Thorne had to confront the gun-quick top-hand Striker—and reveal the secret of his own past!

PUMA PISTOLEERS
By Lee Floren

PRICE $1.95   LB920
CATEGORY: Western

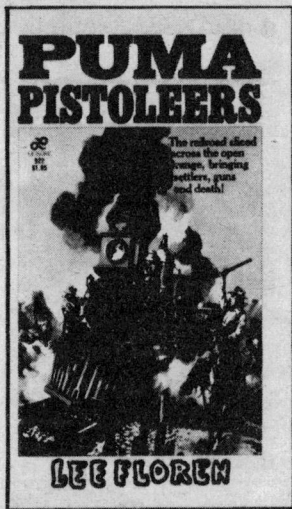

PLOWS AND POWDERSMOKE

Paul Malone and Pete Glenn, two big ranchers, didn't take too well to the small farmers who were arriving by train—so they began gunning them down. Cal Rutherford was hired to protect the farmers, and soon Cal stood alone, with his .45 and a will of steel!

SUNDANCE #38: DRUMFIRE
By Peter McCurtin

PRICE: $1.95 LB976
CATEGORY: Western

SUNDANCE AND GERONIMO!

Apache chief Geronimo was released from a Florida prison camp on the condition that he must become a farmer in Oklahoma. It was up to Sundance to get the hated chief there alive. Their journey was destined for blood.

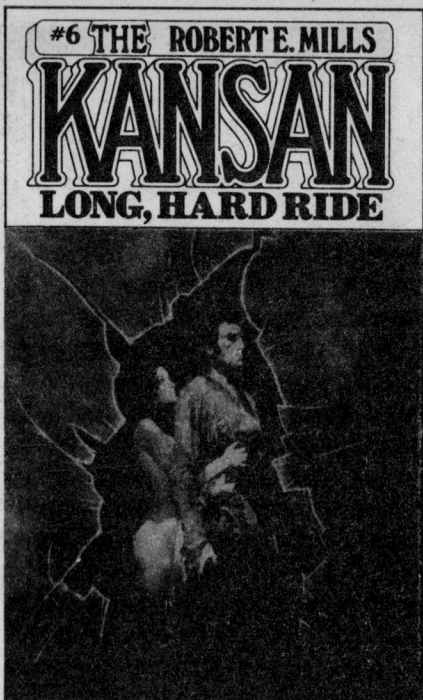

#6 THE ROBERT E. MILLS
KANSAN
LONG, HARD RIDE

THE KANSAN #6: LONG, HARD RIDE
By Robert E. Mills

PRICE: $2.25 LB989
CATEGORY: Adult Western

EAGER WOMEN AND KILLING MEN

The Kansan's long chase begins when he learns that Deanna has left with the ruthless and deadly John Hartung. After a powdersmoke hell on the St. Louis docks, the Kansan continues his hard trail to New Orleans, where he finds the pleasure of old flames and the pain of hot lead!

SUNDANCE #39:
BUFFALO WAR
By Peter McCurtin

PRICE: $1.95 LB990
CATEGORY: Western

WAR CRIES!

Josiah Moore's ruthless and well-armed hunting expedition had invaded the Staked Plains to kill off the last of the buffalo herds. But their presence on the Indian land threatened to explode into war. General George C. Crook needed Sundance's help to avoid the war.

SEND TO: LEISURE BOOKS
P.O. Box 511, Murry Hill Station
New York, N.Y.   10156

Please send me the following titles:

Quantity	Book Number	Price
_____	_____	_____
_____	_____	_____
_____	_____	_____
_____	_____	_____

In the event we are out of stock on any of your selections, please list alternate titles below.

_____	_____	_____
_____	_____	_____
_____	_____	_____
_____	_____	_____

Postage/Handling _____

I enclose..... _____

FOR U.S. ORDERS, add 75¢ for the first book and 25¢ for each additional book to cover cost of postage and handling. Buy five or more copies and we will pay for shipping. Sorry, no C.O.D.'s.

FOR ORDERS SENT OUTSIDE THE U.S.A., add $1.00 for the first book and 50¢ for each additional book. PAY BY foreign draft or money order drawn on a U.S. bank, payable in U.S. ($) dollars.

☐ Please send me a free catalog.

NAME _____
(Please print)

ADDRESS _____

CITY _____ STATE_____ ZIP _____
Allow Four Weeks for Delivery